LOST IN THE

FOREST OF

MECHANICAL

BIRDS

LOST IN THE FOREST OF MECHANICAL BIRDS

— STORIES —

CHRISTIAN MOODY

DZANC
BOOKS

2580 Craig Rd.
Ann Arbor, MI 48103
www.dzancbooks.org

Library of Congress Cataloging-in-Publication Data Available on Request

ISBN 9781938603358
First edition: October 2025
Cover and interior artwork by Margaret Kimball
Interior design by Michelle Dotter

These stories have been appeared, sometimes in different forms, in the following magazines and anthologies:

Best American Fantasy (selected by Jeff Vandermeer), *The Cincinnati Review*, *The Collagist* (selected by Matt Bell), *Alaska Quarterly Review*, *New Stories from the Midwest* (selected by Antonya Nelson), *Best New American Voices* (selected by Dani Shapiro)

Printed in the United States of America

10   9   8   7   6   5   4   3   2   1

For Stella & Forrest

CONTENTS

THE GO SEEKERS

5

HORUSVILLE

35

LOST IN THE FOREST OF MECHANICAL BIRDS

55

THE BABYCATCHER

67

RAY OF GOLDEN YOLK, A NOVELLA

81

THE GO SEEKERS

IN THE FINAL WEEKS OF SIXTH GRADE the world is abloom, the sunset is late, and the game is a daily after-school frenzy that lasts deep into dusk. George and Elise hide beneath a garden gazebo, in a broom closet under a staircase in the historical society, in a long-abandoned tree house littered with disintegrated nudie magazines, and in a tarpaulin-draped canoe afloat in a rickety lakeside boathouse. Once, George and Elise spend the afternoon hiding in the TV room of an elderly widow who suddenly claps her hands at 5 p.m., serves them milk and cookies, and tucks them into the bed of a dusty room filled with rabbit dolls and balls of yarn. They crouch behind chimneys on roofs. They dig holes overnight, cover them with grass, leaves, and branches, and hide in them with juice boxes and crackers the following day. They spend every morning for a week constructing what they call the Movable Bush Suit, a giant shrub they wear around their waists, inside of which they creep from yard to yard. They learn by heart the attics of their neighborhood, the crawlspaces, undersides of porches, hollowed-out trees, drainage culverts, and cobwebbed corners of backyard barns: a world within a world where they learn to live in the quiet and shadow.

In each hiding place, George is aware of the discreet way Elise moves and breathes in the dark. Her elbow taps his ribs. It lasts a few minutes. He can't remember when it first started. It has built up slowly in the darkness, and now it's as much a part of their hiding as holding their breath when a seeker steps near.

On the first official day of summer vacation, George and Elise lie side by side beneath the school stage on an Unofficial Hide, and George realizes that Elise is touching herself. Above them, fairytale scenery from the year's final production sits on the stage: a gingerbread house, a castle, a troll bridge. The curtain is drawn, the auditorium dark. George feels the familiar light tap of Elise's elbow against him. *Touch yourself* is a new phrase to George, something he picked up from an older kid or song or movie, and until now he hasn't understood what it means and still doesn't entirely connect it to what he himself does at night.

"Why do we do Unofficials?" he whispers.

Elise's elbow pauses.

"Unofficials are my favorite," she says quietly.

Unofficials are what they call it when they hide without a game happening, without anyone looking for them. Hiding for the sake of hiding. Elise's elbow patters against him again. He wants to ask why she likes Unofficials so much, but instead he lies in the dark and listens to her breathe. He wonders if it has to do with her mom, who simply up and left when she was still a baby, but he knows the question is off limits. He's tried before.

George sometimes thinks about death when they're lying together in the darkness. He also thinks about whether or not Elise will fall in love with him and marry him when they're older. He believes that she will, that maybe this is what the game is all about—about being with Elise.

"Is it because, you know, your mom?" he asks.

Her elbow pauses. "Unofficials are even quieter than a game," she whispers. "I like how some sounds are far off. Cars. People's voices. Wind. And other sounds are close. Like your stomach, or when the wood planks of the stage creak for no reason. The whole world feels small, like it's forgotten you."

They breathe quietly in the darkness. Eerily, the stage creaks. Elise stills. "Do you think maybe someone stepped on that plank days or years ago, and it's just now lifting up?"

"The creak?"

"Yes."

"Maybe."

Her elbow starts up again. George hears Elise's father, the custodian for the combined school buildings, buffing the floors in the far-off high school hallways. He wonders if Elise hears it too or if parent sounds are invisible, like the hum of your own refrigerator, or your heartbeat.

George likes Elise's dad. He lets them roam the empty school and hide wherever they'd like while he works. Getting to know the classrooms and hallways in their quiet, empty state has made it easier for George to survive in them when they are full.

"Why do you hide with *me*?" he asks her.

It's a long time before she answers. Their conversations while hiding are always like this; minutes and minutes can go by between sentences. It's George's favorite way of talking, as if there is all the time in the world.

"You've always been part of my hiding, from the very beginning. Do you remember the leaves?"

"I don't know, maybe."

She describes it to him, her first memory of hiding. Even though he doesn't remember it, he begins the process of turning it into his own memory: They huddle together under a heap of raked leaves on Elise's front lawn. They are three years old and next-door neighbors. The pleasant smell of autumn decay reminds them of Elise's father's spice cabinet, of the pumpkins, squashes, and gourds on his kitchen counter. The crinkly pile scratches and tickles George's skin, and so do Elise's lips against his ears. "Shh," she whispers. Her dad dumps another wheelbarrow load on top of them. Their shoulders move up and down with laughter.

"Hey, what's under there?" jokes Elise's dad.

They laugh harder. George wants to burst up through the oranges and yellows. Elise holds him still, in a tight embrace, like she still does when a seeker steps close.

"I think I might remember," he tells her now in the understage darkness. Elise's breath quickens. She shivers. From now on, Elise's memory of the leaf pile will be as vivid to George as if it were his own.

Years from now, after the tragedy, everyone will think back to Elise's mother's abrupt absence, to Elise's many hiding escapades, her vanishing acts, and it will all become portentous in retrospect, a series of foreboding omens. Only George will remember the pile of leaves, Elise's breath, the way her elbow moves in the dark.

•

A few weeks later, in June of summer break, the game surges, swells, and swarms through the neighborhood. George and Elise type up House Rules. All players must read, sign, date, and return a copy. Teams of hiders form, teams of seekers form. The teams have mascots. While everyone has to share in both the hiding and the seeking, each team has a tendency, a specialty. It's a difference that seems to be deep down in everyone. The Webelos Scouts are seekers, and when they seek they do so in full uniform, carrying their homemade felt flag with a flaming arrow on it. The flag's forked tongues of fire are always peeling off and getting glued back on. Seekers tend to be like this, with their emblems and badges. They like to be seen and heard. They like you to know they are coming.

The Webelos' younger counterparts, the Daisies and Bobcats, are hiders, and their mascot is the poison dart frog. With a marker, they draw their frog insignia in secret places: ankle, wrist, armpit, shoulder blade, bottom of the left foot. The older D&D kids are hiders too. They play in hooded Druidic robes. You can't tell them apart. They favor dark hiding places where they whisper to each other in Old Elvish. The D&D kids are the ones who develop the dice-rolling system that George and Elise include in the House Rules 2nd edition, the first illustrated edition. The dice—twelve-sided, twenty-sided, and the strangely triangular four-sided die—determine which teams will hide each round, which teams will seek, and what the count will be. The probability is not equal: seeking teams mostly seek, hiding teams mostly hide, and the count is usually around one hundred. But a little randomness in the universe is necessary, and so sometimes hiders seek, seekers hide, and the count is under ten. The way the rules are rigged, George and Elise almost never seek, and when they hide they always hide together. They are a team of two, no mascot, no name. Their motto is silence, their insignia invisibility.

College kids home for the summer form their own teams, roughly divided into state school kids (hiders) and private school kids (seekers). There is a team of seeker-parents who bring their six-year-olds, even though everyone can see the adults are in it for their own deep-seated reasons. There is a team of newly single forty-year-old women from a nearby suburb who just don't give a shit. Their mascot is the flask they pass back and forth in the dark. The teams assemble near the elementary school playground at 11 a.m. Sometimes the games last until midnight, until all the kids in the neighborhood have missed curfew and are grounded. George and Elise ask Elise's dad to drive them to a copy shop to have the third edition of the rulebook printed and bound. By July a fourth edition is printed with new cover art and a password-protected website that includes stats: top hiders, top seekers, and play-by-play accounts of the most legendary and epic games. The House Rules offer extra Advancement Points to the team that finds George and Elise. It's called the Find the Founders Rule. They hide together high in trees and deep in the toolsheds of retired old men who look baffled by the temporary alliance of divorcees and young Druids trampling through yards in search of a place to hide.

By sophomore year of high school they are the Go Seekers, an official club. At their inaugural meeting in the school library, George reads the Tennyson poem "Ulysses" out loud by candlelight. "Come, my friends," he reads, his face flickering above the flame. "'Tis not too late to seek a newer world." Outside, dark clouds rumble. The club members whistle and hoot. George feels like a miniature rock star. He's not sure what his English teacher would say about the poem, or if it even applies to hiding and seeking, but George and Elise and the whole club like the sound of it, and that's enough. He raises and deepens his voice for the thunderous last line, their club motto: "To strive...to seek...to find... and not to yield!" The club cheers. He blows the candle out. A hush falls. Rain drums the roof. In the darkness, students scamper through the high school corridors to hide. Eugene, second vice president of the club and captain of the seekers, begins the official count to one hundred on the principal's intercom. His voice echoes through the begloomed hallways.

By the end of the year Eugene is George's and Elise's best friend and third wheel. Hiders need good seekers, and Eugene is the most persistent seeker they can find. He's also good at recruiting his own kind. Athletes, they realize, have the drive to pursue; they will sweat and suffer to know where you are. Nerds, too, can be tenacious finders, especially those students who stay late after school to conduct lab projects or write research essays. Musicians are especially persistent; they are willing to fail at something over and over, to chase a sound until it is perfect, and chase it farther until it is art. Eugene has all three seeker qualities: math, pole vault, piano. Like George, Eugene is in love with Elise. He is George's best male friend, and George hates Eugene more than anyone, even if he likes him too.

At high school dances George sits up in the gymnasium bleachers where other kids slurp and suck while making out. He watches Eugene and Elise dance. Eugene will always ask Elise to school dances before George does. This is because Eugene is a seeker and George is not. Sometimes, from a hiding spot deep inside a swarm of anonymous dancers, George watches Eugene and Elise jumping and grinding. He sees how their bodies touch. Over the course of many songs, Eugene always steers Elise right into the middle of the dance floor, where the lights flash the brightest, where the dancers who love their own moves peacock and prance and hope to be seen, Eugene chief among them. George knows Elise hates the lit-up center of the dance floor, but he can see she doesn't hate it as much as she says she does. She's as thrilled as she is horrified.

•

The epic spring break meet of their senior year takes place in the high school and lasts for three days. Of the nine other clubs at the meet, seven are from out of state. They assemble in the gym and go over the rules. George sits next to Elise. She has her game face on. It reveals nothing. On her other side, Eugene is smiling his giant, goofy seeker's grin. Elise will eventually want someone quiet to hide with forever, George tells himself, someone to breathe with in the dark, a family of hiders unhidden only to each other. He tries to believe this. George needs to win this meet: the trophy is a scholarship good for a semester's books and tuition, without which he won't be a freshman in college with Elise come fall. Elise says losing isn't an option; they'll be freshmen together if they have to transfigure into invisible vapor to hide and win. Bringing the national meet to their school was Elise's work, her brainchild, for George. The private school kids are utterly silent as the rules are read. They have special hand signs for communicating. They sit in lotus position and control their breathing. Their uniforms are silky cat-burglar unitards and soft leather moccasins.

The game is on. An hour in, George and Elise sit together in a ventilation duct after crawling on their bellies for a short distance at an excruciating pace. George guesses that they have maybe twelve hours before seekers start to poke their heads up through the vents with flashlights. This hiding spot would be a good short-game strategy, but it's not a viable three-day strategy. They sit at a T in the ductwork. One of the arms of the T is a main tunnel that joins the labyrinth of other tunnels. The other arm of the T is a dead end that sits above the high ceiling of one of the more remote girls' restrooms, where the middle school joins the high school. Footsteps and voices echo through the halls below. A crew of intentionally loud seekers passes beneath them. Beaters, they call these groups. Minutes later they hear a ninja-like sweeper crew following the beaters. The beater-sweeper sequence is a common technique: when the beaters pass, hiders feel safe to shift position, sneak out, or whisper, and then the sweepers sweep them up. Only amateurs fall for it. However, this sweeper crew has three additional solo sweepers who follow minutes apart, after the initial sweep, which makes their initial sweeper group more like a decoy, quasi-beater sweep. This is a good trick. These private school kids from Chicago are smart. George can tell it's them by the whisper of their unitards, by the miasmic cloud of sweaty moccasin leather and feet.

Elise gives George a hand signal when the corridors below are quiet again, and they squirm their way slowly down the offshoot duct to the dead end. Here, a vent looks straight down over the girls' toilets. It smells faintly of cigarette smoke and pee. George wonders what they are doing here, and then Elise swings open a false wall at the dead end, revealing another ten feet of ductwork. They inch inside. Elise swings the wall shut and carefully latches it at the top and bottom. She turns on a tiny, battery-operated nightlight with an underwater scene of fish and seashells. It glows faintly blue, then green, then red.

George knows Elise well enough to show no surprise at this hideout. When Elise reveals something you don't make a big deal, you don't mention it, you pretend not to notice. At the same time,

George feels startled and hurt. It appears Elise has had this secret hiding place for a long time. There is a collection of blankets. A pillow. Packs of cigarettes. Rum bottles, full and empty. A flashlight. There is a stack of *National Geographic* magazines stolen from the library. Elise has torn out maps and photos and taped them to the wall: a diagram of ocean currents, mossy boulders in a forest. The entire ceiling is covered in photographs of women's faces. Some are actually old photographs, stained, creased, and weathered by time. Others appear to have been torn out of magazines.

Elise has also taped up a drawing she made with George in eighth grade, a map of a fantasy world they invented for a novel that they never finished. The Forest of Echoes. The Sea of Sad Memories. The Grief Islands feature Elise's rendition of a humanogriff, a creature they invented after imagining the offspring of a centaur and a hippogriff (both back ends are horses, so it's bound to happen). The humanogriff inherits two enormous, useless humanoid appendages from its father instead of its mother's giant eagle wings. The humanogriff flaps and flaps its gigantic arm-wings, wiggling the huge hands and fingers, but can never lift itself up to fly away from the Grief Islands. The map makes George feel a little better. He has a small presence here.

She turns off the nightlight. They share a cigarette in the dark. It's not a great idea, but the nicotine-stained girls' bathroom below might mask the smoke. Elise turns on a tiny book light with a red bulb and writes in a journal. She hands it to George. This is how they will communicate for the next three days.

My dad helped me make this, it reads. *I've spent every fifth period since seventh grade in here.*

Are we cheating? he writes.

Home team advantage, she writes.

Before bed, they hear other hiders crawl through the duct-work. After they pass, Elise's elbow taps his ribs in that familiar way. She pauses. She takes his hand in hers and sets it on his own crotch, where he's hard. He twitches in surprise. She moves his hand on it, and then she lets go. He goes ahead. She holds his free hand with her free hand. It's never felt so good before as it does now, close to her. He's delirious with it and not thinking clearly when he turns his head and finds her mouth. This is George's first kiss. It's not as he imagined it would be, except that it's with Elise. A minute later she pulls two tissues from a box and hands them to him. None of this feels as weird as it should. George never feels more at home in his body than when he is close to Elise in the dark. Over the next three days, George's second through ninth kisses will be the same as his first.

On day two a team of beaters crawls noisily through the tunnels, followed shortly by another team coming from the opposite direction. Individual sweepers follow each group quietly. One of these is Eugene. They know him by his expensive deodorant and the swish of his exercise pants. He pauses at the T. He might smell them, Elise's brand of cigarettes, her sweat mingled with George's. This is how it should be, George thinks: Eugene close by, but always with a wall between them. After a half hour he moves on.

When they have the book light on, George looks up at the ceiling, at all the women's faces looking down at him. A face in the very middle, in an old photograph, reminds him of Elise.

George writes, *Is this one your mom?* and points to it.

My dad gave it to me, she replies.

Why all of the other faces? he writes back.

Elise turns off the book light. They lie side by side in the dark.

Later that evening they hear caught hiders, now seekers, in the girls' bathroom, peeing lengthy pees. Early in the morning, Elise exits their hideout to squat over the vent and tinkle down onto the floor of the girls' bathroom. She pours George's rum bottle of urine down through the vent for him. They both did a cleanse and a fast before the meet—all the hiders talked about it—but now, on the final day, George has to poop wildly. Eugene crawls by twice more but doesn't stop. As hiders are caught, they go straight to the bathroom, where they fart and moan and sigh with relief.

Elise begins drawing a map in the notebook, and they pass it back and forth, adding topography, naming the cities, lakes, and mountains. This must mean she can tell he is suffering, and she's trying to take his mind off it. She takes the pencil from George and writes: *When I find a photograph that makes me think of her, I tape it up here.*

They work on the map. George knows the best way to get Elise to divulge information is to not ask her, to let her take her own time. Midway through an inscription on a historical statue in the public square of Loomopolis, a city of weavers, clothmakers, and storytellers who live just inland from the Sea of Fog, where the coast meets the Weeping Grasslands, she takes the pencil from him again. *I don't remember her,* she writes, *but I like to look at the photographs and imagine what she's like. If I imagine long enough, then I might get one moment with her, right?*

What is her name? he writes back, even though he knows it's a mistake. *We could find her.*

She closes the notebook, turns off the light.

Finally, at the end of day three, the first horn sounds. They haven't named their world yet. That's always last. The first horn means that the seekers have an hour left.

There's a commotion of activity in the hallways, through the ducts, as the seekers get desperate. Elise grips George in a tight hug, like she often does, to keep them both still and quiet. It's George's favorite feeling in the world.

The second horn sounds, and the game is over. After visiting separate bathrooms, George and Elise run out through the high school doors holding hands and smiling deliriously. There is a large crowd. A band starts up. This is all unexpected. Apparently the national meet made the local paper. George and Elise are the lone hiders remaining. Cheerleaders stand on each other's shoulders.

Tailgaters hold up bratwursts and beer and whoop and yell. Elise's dad sits on the hood of his truck and gives them a shy wave. George sees Eugene's face in the crowd, smiling his big goofy smile with so much sadness behind it that George drops Elise's hand for a moment. She takes it up again and holds both their hands overhead.

She turns to him. "I don't want to ever talk about my mom after this." George nods. "My dad says it wasn't enough for her to live here, married to a janitor. She needed more, a bigger world. I don't want to be like her, but I think maybe I need more too."

Their hands are still raised, the crowd still cheering. George looks at Elise's father on the pickup hood, a quiet man with a kind smile. He taught George how to play chess, is the best cook and gardener in the neighborhood. This photo of George and Elise will be a full spread in the yearbook. They will sign it together for almost everyone.

•

The flagship state research university they all choose is a hider's fantasy, with its monastic, forested campus, footbridges over streams, gazebos in secluded groves, and turreted academic castles creeping with ivy. There are forgotten nooks, crumbling crannies, cloistered corners, hidden corridors, secluded study towers, and remote reading rooms. This is all lucky for George and Elise, who don't have any other options financially. Eugene, who does have many options, is accepted into the university's famed School of Music on scholarship. He will also pole vault and double major in mathematics.

They don't have to start a campus club because they can resuscitate a dormant club still on the books that last met during the seventies. The advisor is Full Professor Frederick Bilgarius of the History and Philosophy of Science Department, a scholar of the second Age of Exploration, especially Darwin's voyage aboard the *Beagle*. He has a hider's face; you can't see much of it beyond the bedraggled gray-and-white beard, stained yellow around the mouth from pipe smoke. His office is high up in a turret with curved windows overlooking the campus hedge maze, which is dotted with statues of fauns, dryads, Silvanus, centaurs, and Bacchus. Students run through the twists and turns below, laughing. George, Elise, and Eugene wait in creaky chairs while Bilgarius digs through one of many tottering, yellowed stacks of paper strewn with nutshells and seeds, corners chewed by mice. Miraculously, he produces the club's original charter, with Bilgarius as founding advisor.

The club is called the Society for Undergraduate Crypsis and Mimicry—or the Cryps 'n' Mims—which will have to do. After much pipe sucking and staring out the window, he agrees to update and amend the rules to what George, Elise, and Eugene have proposed. With one condition: That the most points be awarded for finding Full Professor and Club Founding Advisor Frederick Bilgarius. He signs with a flourish, and when he smiles they see he is missing a canine tooth. He probes the hole with his tongue. Bilgarius provides an impromptu lesson about aggressive mimicry techniques used by advanced undergraduate seekers: The professor crouches on the floor and opens and closes his hands to imitate real and false firefly flashes; he draws a golden orb spider web in yellow whiteboard marker on his window, appearing to capture students in the maze below. Then they are dismissed.

After weeks of practice, during which Bilgarius shows them slides of butterflies that look like leaves, they finally have their first major meet over fall break weekend. Elise and George have discovered the drinking of red wine, and Saturday afternoon they hide sloppily in a bell tower with several bottles and are promptly found by Eugene, who gets drunk with them. When they wake up in a pile it is dark and, according to a note taped to George's chest, everyone is still searching for Full Professor and Founding Club Advisor Frederick Bilgarius. Finally, as dawn breaks Sunday morning, someone sees that a section of the maze is smoking a pipe, and Bilgarius steps forward in an emerald academic robe sewn with hedge clippings, his face and beard leafier than the face of the Green Man carved above the labyrinth's archway entrance.

•

On Christmas Eve, George and Elise hide deep inside the Waltham Rare Manuscript Library. They've been here since the December 22 Solstice Hide-and-Seek Meet, a twelve-hour meet, noon to midnight. No one should be looking for them now except for Elise's new boyfriend and George's new girlfriend. They have both been dating an almost-significant other for about a month now, and they've both been prematurely invited home for Christmas to meet the family. If George were going to make it to Christmas Eve at his girlfriend's, he needed to start driving four hours ago. If Elise were going to make it to her boyfriend's, she needed to have shown up for her flight the day before. Breaking up is new to George, but he's hidden with Elise through any number of her breakups so he knows how it's done.

This is the most comfortable hiding ever. They have wine, snacks, several board games in progress, and the gas fireplace is set to its highest crackle in the Waltham Family Foundation Game Archive, a walnut-paneled room with leather sofas, multiple game tables, and rare games from the ancient and modern worlds under glass. The playable, less-rare games are in the walnut cupboards, which is where Elise and George hid themselves during the twelve hours of the Solstice Meet, and also during two hours of the librarians' annual Christmas Party, after which they squirreled away leftover wine and hors d'oeuvres before the custodian cleaned it up.

In the locked and alarm-protected rooms below them a Gutenberg Bible and Shakespeare folio reside behind glass. There is a main reading room, where on non-holidays visiting scholars wear white archival gloves to read the letters of the Romantic poets. There is also a book bindery, repair studio, administrative offices, a staff break room, and endless rows of subterranean, climate-controlled stacks, where Elise and George initially planned to hide before they found the elevator to the Waltham Family Foundation Game Archive.

They spread dozens of boxes throughout the room, shuffle cards, set up spinners and dice, unfold boards, and place pieces in starting positions. They amend rules, and all the games become part of one large drinking game. They rotate through standards: Clue, Risk, Scotland Yard. They also play a naval game they don't quite understand, although they adore the intricate wooden ships with names like *l'Astrolabe* and *La Boussole*, and the map is beautifully illustrated with leviathans and mermaids. When you land on one of these sea monsters you have to take a double drink and remove an article of clothing. Before long they are down to their underwear and a few odd, errant items—a belt, a sock, a mitten— and are almost aware of what they intend to get into when they push away sofas to unroll the giant map that is Twister: Mythological Edition. This version of Twister features a minotaur in a labyrinth, along with Scylla, Charybdis, Circe, and sirens. When Elise half-attempts to crabwalk herself from smoldering Troy to the Oracle at Delphi she bumps George in the mouth with her crotch. They laugh. George is in love again, still. They collapse together, laughing, and without thinking he grabs her hips and kisses his way slowly up her stomach to her mouth, sets himself between her legs. It's George's first time.

"I'm sure we're both very single by now anyway," Elise says hours later, before they have sex again.

•

For their freshman year Spring Break Invitational, the Cryps 'n' Mims organize their biggest game yet. The far-flung members of their former high school club the Go Seekers forego spring breaks on beaches in Florida and Mexico and instead arrive on the slowly thawing campus for a real rager of a hide-and-seek. They bring new friends from their new clubs at their new universities. Even the Druids show up, their robes a little high off the ground now and faded. They've been studying video game design at art school or doing computer things at MIT and Stanford. When they converge for a group hug, their robes appear to blend into a single brown tent supported by a dozen pale, sandaled stick feet.

The groups now all have their own House Rules, so some arguing and compromising ensues. Elise stands on the Speaking Rock in the middle of campus. The rock splits a little brook that flows to either side. She answers questions, and the Druids act as scribes, taking down the rules.

"Name the boundaries," someone says.

"It's the campus map. You can't step foot off campus. You have to be on university-owned property at all times."

"Including, like, by air? By like hot air balloon?" someone says.

"Some part of your body has to always be touching the campus," she says.

"What if you, like, leap off the ground or climb a tree?" someone says.

"I think I've been clear enough," she says. "If a tree is on campus then you're on campus. Is it clear enough?"

The crowd shouts, "Yes!"

A representative of the Druids hands the scroll up to Elise on the Speaking Rock, and she reads the rules out loud. Everyone has agreed that this most epic of games won't have a time limit. Instead, George and Elise, in a nod to the original game in the original neighborhood, are to be like the golden snitch in a quidditch match: the game will only end when they are caught, and they are worth 150 points while other hiders are worth 10. This special rule requires the agreement and signature of Full Professor and Founding Advisor Frederick Bilgarius, who consents to being worth 11 points so long as whoever finds him buys him an immediate eight pints of ale.

"If they find us first, we're coming for you, Professor," say the Druids, each holding a flagon.

The professor tongues his tooth gap. "I'll be waiting," he says, and dons the hood of his emerald robes.

The "golden snitch rule" makes George nervous, since there are so many expert seekers here, all of whom will be looking for them. On one hand, there's a collective desire in the crowd to honor the original neighborhood game, which is nice. At the same time, George senses an even bigger desire to take him and Elise down for good, to end the myth and legend of their hiding skills. As far as he knows Elise doesn't have a secret compartment in an air duct anywhere. And yet, when he looks up at Elise reading the scroll on the Speaking Rock, she is smiling. She's radiant. She lives for this. If George and Elise aren't found, read the rules, then the game continues, no matter how long it takes. Whoever is on campus will search for the week, and whoever can travel back weekends will search on weekends. The game only ends when both are found.

A silence falls while a Druid shakes the D&D dice in a cup. The Druid pours, and the dozens of colorful and variously shaped dice clink and clatter into a tray. There is a collective gasp. The nearly impossible has happened: George is named a seeker and Elise is not. The dice are checked and re-checked. There is less than a 1 in 10,000 chance of George and Elise ever being separated. Yet, here it is. To make matters worse Eugene is a hider, and Eugene can't hide his wide-eyed grin about it, the chance to tuck himself close to Elise for a full week or longer. The rules are amended, and a Druid reads the newly amended article out loud, naming Eugene and Elise as the golden snitch. There's an air of disappointment, since the opportunity to take down the original Dream Team is gone. And yet, everyone knows that the true hider is Elise. She's the one to get.

"Good luck, my friends," George tells Eugene and Elise on a footbridge over the stream near the Speaking Rock. The three hug each other. "I'll be looking for you."

They turn to leave—George to the statue of Odysseus on the seekers' side of the brook, for the count, and Eugene and Elise to the Lightning-Struck Oak on the other side of the brook, the point from which all hiders will depart.

"Wait," says George. He knows he's making a mistake. He stands at his end of the bridge, they pause at their end. "Elise, I love you," he says. "I've always loved you." He looks her in the eyes, but she has her hider's face on and he can't tell what she's thinking. Eugene looks stung. George turns and runs to the statue of Odysseus, heart pounding. He considers foregoing the game altogether. In the twilight, wearing a seeker's blindfold, he stands on the statue's plinth: "To find, to seek, and not to yield!" he exclaims. He blows the candle out, followed by silence—the non-sound of expert hiders hiding, seekers listening. In unison, they chant out loud to one hundred and eleven.

                                  •

George doesn't abandon the game. He's on a quest. The thought of Elise and Eugene together has made a true seeker of him. After a mere six hours, he discovers the Druids huddled in a hollowed-out tree in the campus forest. The next morning, he finds the former Chicago prep school kids, the ones who are now at Princeton, in the guise of hairnet-clad recycling sorters in the dining hall. The ones who are now at Yale—never much for hiding—are in the Music Library playing cards, singing *a cappella*, and eating cheese and crackers. By Wednesday, only Eugene, Elise, and Professor Bilgarius remain. On Thursday, a mud-caked professor Bilgarius emerges from the pond in the campus meadow with a reed in his mouth. He sits down on the grass and asks for an ambulance. He'll be on medical leave for the rest of the semester.

Friday night there is a party, and the mood has changed from one of seeking to one of getting drunk and waiting. "E & E" is what people are calling them for short. They've already achieved a new hiding record. George, who has barely slept, imagines them in the dark, touching each other. He leaves the party wildly drunk, wide-eyed with heartbreak. Late Saturday morning the campus police find him naked in the grotto of the campus hedge maze with an out-of-town seeker he doesn't know. "You called me Elise all night," she tells him. "But you better not call me Elise now." The campus cops issue him a first-warning citation. Still a little drunk, he searches the campus woods alone.

When the week is over, some visiting teams stay an extra few days, sleeping on dormitory floors and common room couches. Professor Bilgarius emails from his recovery room to tell the club to cooperate with campus police. He's CC'd top administration. The campus police investigate, and it turns out that Eugene has mailed a postcard to his parents, telling them he is OK. He has also unenrolled for the semester. Elise has done neither of these things, but of course she wouldn't. They're shooting for two weeks, the club members speculate. They're going for a month, they speculate later.

•

Two weeks back into classes, George is surprised to see Professor Bilgarius—who is supposed to be on medical leave—cross the stage of George's History of Evolution lecture in his emerald robes. The original professor has suffered a full-on heart attack and will need bypass surgery, Bilgarius explains from the podium, whereas he, Bilgarius, has merely suffered some hypothermia, angina, and humiliation from wading in cattails for nearly a week while sucking air from a reed tube underwater. "Medical leave?" he says, and then sticks out his tongue and blows a raspberry. "Discussing crypsis with bright young minds is the best medicine there is."

After that first lecture George finds himself at Bilgarius's office hours several times a week. The professor is content to smoke his pipe up in his turret and mumble and mutter behind his beard and robes, so long as George brings him chocolate, cheese, and strong ale. George tells the old man, many times over, the whole story from the beginning: the pile of autumn leaves, Elise's little arms around him. The hiding place—the ceiling of possible mothers—in the air ducts. Sex in the Waltham Family Rare Games Archive. The misguided declaration of love on the footbridge. The professor blows large smoke rings into the air and then sends small rings through the bigger ones. His missing canine has been fixed and his teeth gleam, something he must have done while on medical leave. They hug at the end of every session, with nary a word from Professor Bilgarius. The old wizard's arms are surprisingly strong and sturdy under the emerald robes.

The more advanced students complain that Bilgarius's lectures are merely chapters read out loud from his books *Love Among the Mimetic Weeds, The Milk Snakes of Mexico and Me,* and *Fly Orchid, My Heart,* all bestsellers in the eighties, but George doesn't mind at all. He enjoys the bearded lull of the professor's familiar voice, and because George is awake all night, searching his mind for Eugene and Elise, the professor's lectures are one of the few times he actually sleeps. Then, exactly one month to the day the seekers chanted to 111, Professor Bilgarius is in the middle of a digression about female hyena pseudo-penises in a lecture that started out as a treatise on Müllerian mimicry in monarch butterflies, when he abruptly stops speaking. There is a long pause. He scans the auditorium with piercing eyes from his podium. "Hiding," he whispers in the parched voice of someone adrift at sea. The students lean forward in their chairs. The hush in the auditorium wakes George up, and he leans forward with his peers to listen. "Hiding," says Professor Bilgarius again. He sighs deeply. "I'm too tired. I can't anymore." He closes his book with a thump. He leaves the stage and walks up the center aisle toward the doors at the back. He pulls his emerald robe up over his head and drops it on the floor, tears off his beard, and it is Eugene in a white T-shirt and blue boxer shorts who exits the auditorium.

•

Later, after the police and campus administration have questioned Eugene at length, George and Eugene have a beer in a pub frequented by the older professors. Eugene has been drinking here as Professor Bilgarius for a month. The bartender doesn't even ask for their fake IDs.

"She wouldn't hide with me," says Eugene. "Because I'm not you, I guess. When I asked her to marry me, she told me if I could last longer than her in the game she'd consider it."

George wants to punch him. "You proposed?"

"You declared your love first. You spoke the unspoken. We've both loved her forever. What was I to do?"

"I've loved her longer."

Eugene shrugs. "Now I've lost her. I failed. She knew I would fail."

"A proposal would only guarantee that she would never marry you," says George. "Do you know her at all? Telling her I love her was the dumbest thing I've ever done."

Eugene shrugs. "I wear my heart on my sleeve," he says. "Apparently, so do you."

They sip beer. George wants to fight him, considers fighting him. But Eugene also feels like his closest link to Elise, like the only friend George has, which is exactly what Eugene is.

Eugene's story is this: he hid in Bilgarius's office, prepared with an emerald robe and beard he'd procured way back at the fall meet, waiting for the moment the dice would choose him as a hider. He'd long suspected that if he proved he could be a hider to Elise, she might love him. He knew Bilgarius's turret wasn't ideal concealment, but then again no one would think to look for Bilgarius there, and if they "found" Eugene as "Professor Bilgarius," Eugene's plan was to join the seekers and technically still be hidden and unfound. He'd reveal himself the moment Elise was found, and then she'd love him, and so on. It seemed brilliant, to Eugene. As it turned out, no one from the game looked in the turret. The cleaning crew treated Eugene like Bilgarius when they emptied the trash at night, and colleagues—perhaps getting news from the custodians—wound their way up the turret stairs to inquire about his health. Eugene answered them with mumbles and a thumbs up. When a colleague came down with a heart attack, the department head asked Bilgarius—since he was on campus already and seemed in good health—if he'd return from medical leave and fill in.

"It was so lonely," says Eugene. He sips a fresh pint. He reaches out a hand to touch George's shoulder, hesitates, pats George, then grips his shoulder like a miniature, one-handed hug. "Our talks together meant a lot to me. You saved me with your company, I think. And your cheese."

George thinks about fighting him again, but instead grips Eugene's shoulder back. "I was so jealous," says George.

"I know, you told me, told 'Bilgarius,'" says Eugene. "Elise said that if I didn't out-hide her, she'd marry you instead. She said it was what she'd always planned."

George drinks deeply from his mug and searches Eugene's eyes for the truth. Eugene's never been a liar and doesn't look like a liar now. Eugene stands up and extends a hand. "Congratulations," he says.

George laughs, nearly spitting out beer, and waves away the handshake. "You're drunk," he says. "Elise was joking. She was fucking with you."

George believes what he's saying, but he also doesn't want to. Of course they would marry each other. The leaf pile, the darkness beneath the stage, the Games Archive. What else is marriage but the person you most want to hide with? He believes it, and he doesn't.

"We'll find her. You two will be together," says Eugene, a tear sliding down the side of his nose.

George smiles, squeezes Eugene's shoulder with another one-handed hug. "We won't be together anytime soon," says George. "Maybe when we're ancient, like forty years old. Elise isn't going to settle down for a while. She hides from one relationship by jumping into another one. She likes sex with a lot of different people. She could have been with any number of people since the countdown. Let's find her."

"Let's find her," says Eugene, lifting his beer. They knock their mugs together.

The two friends don't so much look for Elise as wander campus and wait for her to reveal herself in the way of her choosing. George stands on his Footbridge of Embarrassment in the middle of campus, the brook trickling beneath it, and he thinks of a home with Elise. On the beach, their children splash through foamy fingers of surf. On the deck of a mountain home, George and Elise drink coffee and watch mist weave through the evergreens. On a boat somewhere in Scandinavian waters, they peer at fjords through binoculars, Elise's belly pregnant with their first child. It is dusk and fireflies twinkle across campus when George realizes that Eugene has already said goodnight and left him alone on the bridge. Some of the firefly blinks are mating calls. Others are the false flashes of predators. His heart feels insane.

•

Dogs are brought in to sniff the campus when Elise is declared a real missing person. Her face is on posters. Police interview all the seekers and hiders at length, again and again. The search continues through summer, with seekers of a different sort volunteering from all across the country. They spread their arms, touching fingertips, and walk the campus, the town, and the neighborhood back home.

News of the disappearance spreads across the Internet and hide-and-seek takes on a new popularity among teens, who feel the twinkle of danger and sex when they read about it online. Elise is on T-shirts. Her face becomes an Internet meme that has her hiding in the most ridiculous places. George worries that Elise will see these things and never come out. Internet infamy is her worst nightmare, a life she couldn't live. It could be years before she emerges, or forever. He believes, in his heart, that she's still hiding, that she's a master, that this is what she does. He imagines her sipping wine in a secret room behind a painting in the university art museum. He imagines her attending classes under a new identity she's been building for years. He imagines her in a foreign city, starting over, gone, hiding forever. Maybe she's found her mother and reunited. When he walks the campus with Eugene at the start of their sophomore year he finds himself following the smell of decay through the woods. He follows it all the way to a dead fawn. He lifts it with a big branch and looks under it, just to be sure.

•

Throughout the year George searches for Elise. He lifts manhole covers at night and descends ladders beneath streets and sidewalks. He spelunks the university's sewers and underground conduits with a headlamp affixed to his forehead. He sleeps in late and dreams of her stuck in tight places. He wakes up in a sweat, fighting his covers. Eugene transfers schools. In his last email to George he writes, *Please don't contact me again. It's too painful, and I've moved on.* Ignoring him, George writes and texts, asking for help with the search, certain that his messages aren't getting through. Eugene blocks him on Facebook, across all social media.

George visits Professor Bilgarius several times per week, like he did when Bilgarius was Eugene in disguise. Bilgarius listens, nods, and smokes his pipe, and when there is nothing more for George to say they stand at the turret windows, sip liquor, and stare down into the hedge maze. Bilgarius gives George study abroad brochures: "Leave," says Bilgarius. "Go see places. Free your mind." He also gives George articles and books on crypsis and mimicry, on the history of natural history, and on Darwin's voyage aboard the *Beagle*. George reads them carefully many times over, hoping Bilgarius has given them to him because hidden somewhere within is secret information about Elise. He knows this is fantasy, but George has run out of physical places to look and combing through texts satisfies his drive to search. He sifts through data. He finds overlooked connections. He seeks the words and meanings hidden behind other words and meanings. This academic work calms his mind, like doing a puzzle. His GPA goes up. He finds a home here, in his homework, and he shies away from parties, from football games, from people. It feels like hiding and searching at the same time.

•

In the summer George stays in the college town and works on a lawn care crew. He peeks into sheds. He stomps on the grass for signs of a hidden trapdoor. He spits on basement windows to rub away grime and peer in. If Elise is captive somewhere, she knows George will look forever. The idea could be keeping her alive.

"I'm looking for you," he whispers to Elise before he sleeps.

"What?" says a temporary lover, next to him in bed.

Junior year, George calls Elise's dad and asks for evidence that Elise was once real and not just a mental construct, an imaginary friend. The first time he calls, Elise's dad gives him detailed lists of memories and reasons, and they laugh and cry together. The second and third times, Elise's dad hangs up.

•

Professor Bilgarius insists that George not enroll in the graduate program in the history and philosophy of science. He encourages George to skip graduate school altogether and to head out into the world to make money, shake things up, and live a simple and happy life. George doesn't listen, and in the second year of graduate school he teaches his own discussion section, and in the third year he teaches his own lecture. George sometimes stops mid-sentence to examine the faces of his students, to see if she's there, hiding under his nose. The students don't understand it, but they like it. They find it dramatic and piercing. *Have I have found you, Elise?* he sometimes writes in the margins of term papers. There are rumors among his students that he's been seen in strange places: Astraddle steeply pitched rooftops with a drink in hand, up in tree branches smoking a cigarette, emerging from manholes covered in grime, lying beneath porches, asleep on a sofa in the Waltham Family Game Archive late at night. All the rumors are true.

George gives up on Elise. She is lost. He gives up looking for her monthly. He gives up weekly. He stands in Bilgarius's office and promises to give up by the next quarter-hour chime of the campus clock, and with each new chime he promises again.

•

The day before the final exam for George's lecture class, George gets a phone call from Elise's father. George has been calling the house from time to time, but he always hangs up before Elise's dad can pick up the phone.

"I won't call you anymore. I won't," George answers.

"It's okay," the man says. "We need to meet."

"No, I promise I won't call anymore."

"Do you have a car?"

"Yes, but I usually take the bus home to save on gas. I could come this weekend."

"I'll see you tomorrow evening. I'll text when I'm on campus."

George tries to reply and confirm but nothing comes out. The man hangs up.

•

It's dark, past dinnertime, when Elise's dad pulls up in front of the student union. George gets in the pickup. They shake hands awkwardly. They start driving. A few turns later they have left the college town and are driving down a dark country road. Elise's dad has finally lost it, George thinks. He blames George for Elise's disappearance and is going to murder him on some back road.

"Look," says George. "I don't know anything."

"I know you don't."

They keep driving. The dark road is long and straight, empty cornfields and patches of woods to either side. George quietly unclicks his seatbelt and places his hand on the door latch, in case he has to roll out. A few miles farther, Elise's dad abruptly slows down, clicks on his right blinker, and turns into a dirt tractor lane between fields. They slowly bump down the lane about a hundred yards, and then he turns the truck off. It's quiet. Wind blows over the bare fields. The engine ticks and cools.

"Why are we here?" says George. He is ready to run out across the fresh-tilled dirt if he needs to.

Elise's dad takes a deep breath. "I didn't mean to drive this far. I couldn't decide if I should tell you what I know. It's the right thing for you, but maybe not for me."

George looks at the man, but the man stares down the tractor lane, searching the darkness with his eyes. The moon appears from behind a cloud and bathes the field in its light. George looks out the window, imagines tiny seeds under the dirt, roots and shoots pushing their way out.

"Here," says Elise's dad, and he hands George a folded piece of paper.

George opens it, looks at it by moonlight. It's a photo of Elise printed in color on a cheap home printer. She's sitting close to a handsome man with salt-and-pepper hair, a baby on her lap. Two things feel wrong with the picture. One, Elise has aged. Two, she's smiling and looks happier than he's ever seen her.

Her dad snatches the photo, opens the truck door, and sets it on fire with a lighter. It warps and blackens. He closes the door. The smell of burning paper lingers.

"Now you know," he says.

"Was that a real photo?" says George.

Her dad smiles while looking ahead out the windshield. "I always thought of photos as hard evidence," he says. "But to you guys—your generation—there's nothing more suspicious."

"I guess so," says George. "She's alive?" He knows it's true. He sees it on her dad's face.

"We've emailed. Talked on the phone once. She's happy."

George nods. He feels numb and doesn't know what to think.

Elise's dad looks George hard in the eye now: "You're to say nothing. Not a thing to anyone. Is this understood?"

George nods.

"Say it's understood."

"I promise I'll never tell."

Her dad's face softens. He places a hand on George's shoulder. "You remind me of her," he says. "You two were always together. All this time I kept telling myself you must already know, probably knew before I did. I'm sorry."

"How long have you known?"

"It was a little over a year after she left, and then one morning she called. It was an answered prayer. She told me that if I told anyone she'd disappear again. I believed her, of course. You're the only one who knows. She's traveled, had a whole life. Maybe found her mother, maybe not. She has a child now, and I think she needs me. She might be changing. Kids will do that to you. I might actually see her again." He pauses to roll down his window. A cold breeze blows through the cab. He looks at George. "Please keep quiet. Don't ruin it. Don't make her go away again."

"I won't."

They sit in silence for a long time, and then Elise's dad starts the engine and backs out of the field. They drive to campus in silence.

"Do you need dinner?" he asks George back at the student union, pulled up to the curb.

"I'm good," says George. It feels too weird, too tense, and he wants the encounter to be over so that he can sit alone somewhere and figure out how he feels. There's only shock now, a kind of numbness.

"Okay," says her dad. "If you change your mind, if you need company, I'm staying here in town tonight." He smiles. "You really were always around," he says. "Always the two of you. It's nice to see you again."

They shake hands. George gets out of the car. He pauses before he shuts the door. "She looks happy," says George. "In the photo. I think she's happy."

"Now you know," says Elise's dad. "Go live your life."

•

George can't sleep that night. He drives back to the old neighborhood. It's 3 a.m. when he parks in the lot of the local grocery chain and walks a mile to Elise's house. His own childhood home next door is dark and quiet, his parents asleep within. He knows how to go from fence to tree to rooftop to upstairs bathroom window, but he doesn't need to. He doesn't even need the key kept in the planter where it's always been. The back door isn't locked.

It's easy to find what he's looking for. It's right there in the messy spare room her dad uses as an office, scattered across a desk, some of it in a manila folder, the rest of it on the computer desktop. She's in Spain. Her husband is Spanish. Elise didn't even take Spanish in high school. She took Latin and French and dabbled very poorly in Japanese. It was like she took everything available except Spanish, and now she's in Spain. George is careful not to disturb anything. He snaps photos with his phone, and he texts himself her address and information. He doesn't want her dad to know, doesn't want Elise to know he's coming. He imagines he'll make it look like an accident, like he happened upon her while on vacation. Or maybe he'll just watch her from a distance to make sure she's as happy as she looks in all the photos he's found. She looks happy in every one.

He stands in her bedroom and loses track of time. On the wall is the framed yearbook photo of the two of them, emerging from the high school halls hand in hand, victorious. Every edition of the House Rules, the maps of the fantasy world they invented together—it's all here. Different scenarios pass through George's mind. He could declare his love, even though it backfired once and he's not even sure he feels it anymore. She's obviously in love with her baby and Spanish husband. He could be angry and confront her, but he's not sure he feels that now either. He could say goodbye to her. He'd like that.

"George?" he hears from downstairs. "Are you here?"

Elise's father must've been sleepless too. His mind must've turned to what he would do in George's position. George gets down on the floor and squeezes under Elise's bed, much more slowly than he did as a child. Elise's dad walks through the house. George lies on his back and listens. Elise's dad is quiet now. He enters the bedroom and stands silently. George imagines Elise squeezing him tight, like she would have long ago. Her dad sits on the bed, and it's several minutes before George realizes the man is crying.

The crying becomes sobbing. Elise's dad collapses onto the covers. His heaves shake the bed.

George has two possible plans in mind. George's first plan is to drive to the airport to see if his credit card can handle a flight to Spain. The second plan is to do nothing, to let her be gone and happy. He's not sure which is better, which he has in him. For now, though, he lies still, listens to Elise's dad cry himself to sleep above him. It feels good to hide again. The man sleeps. George hides. He listens to his own breath, crouched under the leaf pile in his memory. He feels the dry tickle against his skin, smells the scent of autumn decay. Elise's lips whisper against his ear.

HORUSVILLE

Stephen went to the woods instead of math class. His algebra book was still under the backseat of the school bus, or under his bed, or maybe even somewhere in the woods, swollen and muddy from last week's rain. Losing the textbook had meant weeks of calling out answers with squared *Y*s to problems that had no *Y*s, which equaled weeks of the math teacher yanking him into the hallway and yelling at him. It had been easier when his fellow ninth graders laughed and made fun, but now, baffled and full of pity, they avoided eye contact. The obvious solution to math class, the answer he arrived at several times per week, was to take the latest issue of *She-Hulk* from his locker and walk out of the school doors into the dim, shadowy woods, where the sponge-thick and gently bioluminescent moss felt refreshingly cool on his bare feet. He would go to his favorite tree, solemnly turn the carefully dog-eared pages of *She-Hulk*, and jerk off to her muscular green thighs, her bulging green ass.

On his way to fulfill this plan, just a short way from his favorite tree, he saw his art teacher, his big brother's fiancée, naked.

What was immediately attractive about Miss Baskin's nakedness was how She-Hulkishly green it was. The wood's thick canopy of leaves filtered light into a muted jade gloom, and the glimmering moss radiated a faintly emerald glow. It was possible that Miss Baskin's thighs were somewhat muscular, too, and her ass possibly

bulging, although from a hundred or so yards away, the view partially obscured by trees, it was difficult to say. It looked like she was
slow-dancing by herself. She ran her fingers through her long, deep
red hair—a little too red, she'd explained to Stephen's wide-eyed
art class the morning after she'd dyed it, because she'd used a five-
dollar do-it-yourself kit from the clearance aisle. Stephen snuck
closer, moving from trunk to trunk.

As he got nearer he could see that Miss Baskin was dancing
for the tree eyes. She swayed her hips back and forth while the
eyes—the whites especially bright from the recent rain that had
also turned the irises blue—swung to and fro, like pendulums. The
tree eyes, he knew, were why people went to the woods. Prior to
Miss Baskin, Stephen had spied on other people. The former town
mayor, shortly before he died, would come to deliver grandiose
speeches in acceptance of high offices. The high school janitor had
a velvet cape he wore while he failed over and over at sleight of
hand, littering the moss with dropped coins and cards. Stephen
once saw an old lady confess on her knees to acts of sadism so
imaginative and outlandish that, still, on some nights, he wasn't
able to sleep until he convinced himself she'd been lying.

Why people spoke to the trees—which only had eyes, after
all, not ears—Stephen couldn't figure out. He was glad they didn't
have ears; it was bad enough that they were forced to see whatever
anyone showed them. If it were up to him, they'd have mouths and
arms so they could keep people away by screaming obscenities and
throwing their own apples, like the trees in *The Wizard of Oz*. But
these trees didn't have obscenities or apples, just creepily intense
eyes that tracked every movement with the precision of high-tech
security cameras. Some eyes were small as shirt buttons, others big
as dinner plates. Wet and gleaming, with shining irises that varied
in color by tree type and weather, the eyes dappled trunks and
limbs and dangled from twig ends like blinking fruit.

There was a game he played in which he sat still for a very long time until the eyes forgot him. It wasn't the most exciting game, but when the eyes forgot him they opened and closed their nut-shell lids with mesmerizing out-of-sync slowness that made him imagine migratory moths alighted in the woods to rest. Inevitably, he'd get tired and scratch his nose or balls and—*snap!*—every eye would be on him again.

To get closer to Miss Baskin, to really see in detail what he was anxious to see, Stephen had to hop over the tiny double stream that trickled such a sinuous path through the woods that it often ran right alongside itself in opposite directions. He hopped once, twice, then slipped and planted his face in the moss. The tick-tocking eyes rolled around in their sockets to stare at him. When he got back up, she was running. She had an armful of clothes. Her bare shoulder blades jutted. Her bright foot bottoms flashed. Her ass cheeks switched from dimpled to full while she ran. He saw the bumpy line of her spine. Hip bones. The small of her back.

He picked up a sock, a bra, a boot. The sock was brightly striped in yellow, blue, and white, but the bottom was threadbare, just shy of a big hole. Her bra was white but dingy on the straps and edges. He stuck his nose and mouth in each cup and inhaled. When he saw her bloodred boot shining on the moss, he was afraid to touch it. Miss Baskin's daily stumble through the streets to the high school halls was a favorite local spectacle—Stephen had seen the old people shuffle onto their porches before dawn to wait, watch, and whisper. Each tottering step in those boots threatened to send her tumbling into a front yard, where (hopefully) she'd fall onto the grass, her long limbs splayed. Stephen could see it in people's eyes: All of Horusville was ready for the chance to rush forward and help her to her feet, or (even better) to just lie down on the grass beside her. It was obvious from the way no one could look at each other after she passed. There was something embar-rassing about the bloodred boots; they made the whole town pain-fully aware of one another, a community of watchers, so many hearts so alike and so easily stirred. You couldn't blame Miss Baskin for pretending not to notice; it was too much longing for any one person to acknowledge. Her boots were like a talisman that accepted looks on her behalf and reflected them back for what they were: the acute red pang of loneliness, a whole town's worth. Stephen knew he had to give the boot back.

In the graveyard between the woods and the town, Stephen watched Miss Baskin button her blouse. He crouched behind the monument of Anne Lynne Brown, memorialized in the act of presenting her famous green-bean casserole. Miss Baskin almost fell down while trying to put on her panties. She caught herself by placing a hand on the big stone belly of a butcher who had a great steak of black marble in one hand, a giant knife in the other. The grave markers were all life-size statues of dead people posed at occupations or hobbies. Stephen noticed that Anne Lynne Brown's statue had a bronze plaque detailing the casserole recipe.

The story of the statues, as Stephen had heard it in his fourth-grade local history unit, was that Horusville's founders, anxious about what sort of attention the tree eyes might bring, created the elaborate graveyard as a barrier to waylay wanderers. This solution was, however, too successful, since each year ever greater numbers of visitors came in search of the eccentric monuments.

Miss Baskin hopped a few times to zip up her jeans. She must have sensed someone watching, because she darted up and down the rows of statues. Stephen had to dive, roll, and crawl. The sun was setting, and he hid himself in the long shadow cast by a disheveled mechanic with wild hair. Stephen could see the chipped polish on Miss Baskin's toenails; he could hear each breath.

"Asswipe!" she screamed in anger, which sounded so ridiculous that Stephen had to bite hard on the heel of his hand to keep from laughing.

The statues of dead men looked a little too tall and muscular. They posed with oversize objects. A nearly seven-foot farmer stood, like Atlas, with what would have been the world's biggest pumpkin on his shoulders. Almost all of the dead women offered food. There was a waitress who poured coffee from a pot that was also a working fountain. She smiled and smiled in an endless attempt to fill a bottomless cup. The liquid poured straight through the mug into a pool at her feet.

"Masturbator!" Miss Baskin screamed again before walking off braless, with only one boot, one sock. This time the insult hurt, the accuracy of it. Either she was a good guesser or she'd seen him in the woods before, doing what he did at his favorite tree. It had almond-shaped eyes, his tree. They were hazel. They aided his imagination. They made the job less lonely by looking on with what he was sure must have been interest and sympathy. The almond-eyed tree was so consoling that he now loathed masturbating anywhere else, which was partly why he skipped school so often, even before he'd lost his math book.

When Miss Baskin left the graveyard, Stephen visited his parents. In the afterlife, Mr. Blue squinted at a test tube and wore a lab coat. He had frizzled hair, as if electrified. He had been the school's best and dorkiest science teacher. Stephen's mother presented a meatloaf. For weeks after his parents were buried, visitors came to Mrs. Blue's monument, placed tracing paper over the engraved recipe, and copied it down by rubbing over it with pencil. It still startled him to walk down a street in the evening and smell his mother's cooking. For reasons Stephen didn't understand, his parents' monuments were embarrassing to Ed, his much older brother. He suspected Ed's reasons for disapproval were the same reasons he, Stephen, loved them so well.

There was a piece of limestone paper taped to his dad's back, reading KICK ME in an adolescent scrawl. No one would call Mr. Blue a funny man, but students had found his efforts endearing. He'd only had an inch or two added in death, making him one of the shorter men in the cemetery. Next to Stephen's dad was Uncle

McCarty, decked out in thespian tights, neck ruffle, floppy hat, pointed beard. He had been amusing, as far as English teachers went, but for some reason Stephen's dad was the only teacher who liked him, maybe out of a brother-in-law's obligation. A car crash killed all three of them the night Ed beat Stephen seven times in a row at Monopoly.

Stephen stretched out on the grass between his parents, as he often did, and looked up at the sky. He tried to clear his mind and forget that his favorite teacher had apparently seen him jerk off to a comic book and a tree. Slowly, the afterglow faded and the first stars appeared. He remembered how his father and Uncle McCarty would get drunk and reenact Monty Python skits on the front porch. For a moment he thought he heard their voices, their fake accents. But it was only the squawk of geese flying in a V overhead.

•

That evening, Stephen sat right across from Miss Baskin at the round dinner table. Miss Baskin had accepted Ed's marriage proposal, attempt number two, a week earlier. The family had never said grace when Mr. and Mrs. Blue were alive, but Ed insisted grace was just good manners, like elbows off the table. During prayers, especially long prayers like Ed's, which always included his big plans for constructing housing developments, Stephen liked to examine people's faces. Lately he'd been looking at Miss Baskin's face. Miss Baskin never noticed, because she was always examining Ed's face while he prayed about development. Miss Baskin watched closely, with such pained, focused intensity that you'd think Ed's praying face held some crucial clue to Miss Baskin's own life, which Stephen supposed it probably did.

But this evening, when Stephen looked up to examine Miss Baskin's face, Miss Baskin locked eyes with him. Her eyes were hazel and unhappy. For the first time ever he bowed his head and tried to follow his big brother's prayer. Ed, who was also the town's unusually young mayor—not a real mayor, but the kind of mayor who officiated the monthly town meeting in the high school cafeteria—prayed that he would get the contract to expand the Horusville Library, which served both the town and the school. He was courting the favor of Miss Mahogany, the shriveled librarian, whose expertise had great sway in the matter, even though everyone knew she had an entire wall full of rare dirty books. Patrons had been known to attempt to steal the rare dirty books. Miss Mahogany, small as she was—and old, too, with wrinkled skin the same burnished red brown of her name—would beat such would-be book thieves so mercilessly with her yardstick that the pyrotechnic scarves holding her braids together would fly off, and then her hair would whip about so fiercely, all snakelike, that you could imagine the poor recipient of her wrath mistaking her yardstick's crack for the snap of poisoned fangs. Those days, Stephen always felt, were the best days in the library—the only good thing about a research project. However, whenever anyone came from afar to examine one of the few existing copies of some dirty book, Miss Mahogany was attentive and kind and didn't give a damn about whether or not the guest had a library card.

"...and I'm sorry, Lord, that I purchased those rare issues of *The Pearl* and other Victorian erotica and donated them to the library," Ed prayed, and his voice indicated that his prayer was winding down. "Accept my apology also for purchasing and donating the rare set of *My Secret Life*. I didn't read either donation. Not in their entirety. Only a few pages, which I am trying to forget. But some of it rhymes, Lord, and this makes forgetting difficult. I hope they do not end up in the hands of the children, although they probably will, but this concern would really be Miss Mahogany's responsibility. For she is the librarian. Amen."

Rather than raise his head, Ed took advantage of his mouth's proximity to his plate and stuffed it with chicken. "Where are your boots?" he asked his fiancée, his mouth still full.

Miss Baskin was wearing flip-flops. She paused long enough that Stephen could tell she didn't have an answer.

"I'm painting them," he decided out loud. "I'm doing a painting *of* them."

"Why would you do that?" asked Ed in the slightly annoyed, businesslike tone he used for all questions.

"For your engagement present."

He was sure he could feel Miss Baskin's hazel eyes boring into him, but when he looked she was just watching her fork move through her bowl of greens.

"Let's see it."

"The boot or the drawing?"

"Both."

"I only just started. It's a sketch."

Ed shrugged. "Go get it."

Stephen went upstairs to his room, drew on his pad, and brought it down to the table with the boot.

"It's preliminary."

Ed held the drawing at arm's length and rotated it this way and that. While Ed examined it, Stephen realized that it looked a lot like a paramecium. Ed continued to flip and rotate, comparing it to the boot Stephen had placed in the middle of the table. It still looked like a paramecium. He could see it on Ed's face: fear for his little brother and his dim prospects in life. Drawing was Stephen's only known talent, and here he couldn't make a boot look like a boot. Ed's eyes watered.

"It's really good," Ed lied.

For Stephen, this was a perfect moment: his brother's love and pity, out in the open. Ed, with his good business sense, couldn't help but place himself in the role of villain. Whenever Ed acted like an asshole, Stephen thought back to when he was eight and Ed had caught him experimenting with their mother's lipstick. Instead of mocking him, Ed had carefully instructed Stephen in the intricacies of heavy metal makeup. With a red lightning bolt across his face and Ed painted up into a kind of Rabid Cat Man, they played shirtless air guitar to metal anthems and practiced their scowls in the mirror.

"He's actually quite good," said Miss Baskin. Ed was still looking in pain at the paramecium.

"I can tell," he lied again.

"No—I mean, he's much better than this sketch would indicate."

"It shows great promise."

She looked at Stephen now. "I know it will be good after you put more time into it."

When they made eye contact, Stephen didn't see any anger or shame—just his art teacher.

"Keep the boot as long as you need it," she said

"Really?" said Ed. "Stephen, how long will that take?

"Twenty-four hours of hard work," Stephen replied, making the number up on the spot.

Ed nodded thoughtfully. He only accepted firm answers, preferably numerical ones.

•

During lunch, the cafeteria lady with the beehive and biceps let Stephen smoke cigarettes out back by the dumpsters near the loading dock. He didn't like cigarettes very much, but he liked the lunchroom less. The humiliation of algebra class had whittled down his seating options. Today, he was sure, he would remember to look for his math book.

He spotted Miss Baskin on the far side of the parking lot, walking away from the school. She glanced his way, took a few more steps, then stopped and squinted, shielding her eyes from the sun. He waved, forgetting he had a cigarette dangling from his mouth. She waved back and walked away.

During third period, he redrew the sinking of the *Lusitania* by U-boat in pencil on his desk—an intricate drawing that someone, probably the janitor, was always erasing, and so it had to be redone every day. All those little people floating in the water. When the drawing was finished, he filled in the first bubble of his history exam, which glared bright white beneath the fluorescent lights overhead. Then he closed his eyes and dreamed of the wood's jade gloom. Next period, in the crumbling cement cave of the boys' locker room, he dressed in the required red shorts and white shirt. On the wooden basketball court, he performed a series of squat thrusts, push-ups, and sit-ups. He ran the bases during the chaos of indoor kickball and did not stop, bursting out of the metal door and into the school parking lot, past the courthouse square, through the neighborhood of front porches, and into the graveyard, where he took off his shoes and socks to step barefoot onto the glowing moss, into shadow.

The tree eyes, even while they tracked him, blinked out thick, salty tears that made transparent dots on his thin white shirt. It was the weeping time of year, when the trees cry before the leaves crinkle and fall. The chimelike tinkle of drips dropping, leaf to leaf, and plopping onto the moss or the tops of his bare feet was like rain, except slower and possessed of a pleasant sadness that made the crying almost contagious.

Miss Baskin saw Stephen first. She sat naked on the moss in a small clearing, legs pulled tight to her chest. The clearing was all but dry, just a few eyes blinking and dripping from overhanging branches.

"Here's a quick lesson," she said. Her voice was shocking, less sweet than the voice she used in class. "The next time you stand and stare at a naked woman, you might think about saying something. Or doing something. Or at least look her in the eyes. If you just stand there, you come across as a creepy weirdo."

"Sorry." He could feel his face flush. He couldn't think of anything to say. He felt like a creepy weirdo.

"You stole my bra."

"I know."

"It was my only comfortable bra."

He nodded. He tried to keep eye contact, but he wanted to look at her skin—any part of it. It was very fair, and he imagined that if he touched it, it would go flush and then quickly fade to white again. He could almost see her cleavage, but not her nipples—her knees hid them. He could see, just a little, the hair between her legs. Then she pulled her feet and legs in closer, so that he couldn't see between them anymore.

"Well, Stephen, you should give my bra back."

"I tossed it. I didn't want Ed to find it."

"Goddamn," she said, shaking her head. "Well, it's going to be kind of embarrassing for you to buy me a new one, isn't it? Or do you like shopping?"

Stephen thought for a moment.

"Maybe I could just pay you the money and you could order one out of a catalog."

"I guess so. But that wouldn't teach you a lesson, would it? Take off your shirt," she said.

"My shirt?"

"You're the only one who's wearing one."

"Why do you want me to take off my shirt?"

"Because I'm sitting here naked and you're not. And your shirt is already soaked through. I can see your nipples. And why are you dressed like that—are those your pajamas?"

"I ran away from gym class."

She laughed.

"Take off your shirt and sit down," she said, patting the moss beside her. "You came to spy on me. Might as well get a close look and make things even at the same time."

He lifted the wet shirt over his head, but he didn't sit down.

"Take off your shorts, too," she said

She sounded mean. He couldn't tell if she was serious or mocking him. The thing was, he halfway did want to take off his shorts. Right then, a cold breeze caused a shower of tears to shimmer from the leaves overhead. He imagined himself a grown man in a movie, taking off his pants. (They would be pants, of course, and not too-tight gym shorts.) He felt cold and numb. His dick felt small. He felt like a child.

"I'm not going to do that," he said.

"Then go away and stop looking at me."

"It's not the same."

She stood and came close to him. She balanced one hand on his shoulder and lifted her leg to show him her thigh. He shivered.

"Describe it," she said.

He couldn't stop shivering. "It's great," he said.

"What do you see?"

There were veins on her leg that looked erupted, spilled over, and painful.

"Just say what you're thinking."

He had a weird impulse to put his mouth on her thigh.

"Say something, goddammit."

"Purple fireworks," he blurted.

She laughed. "Okay. Like a little celebration happening down there? That's lovely. Before long I'll be a walking bruise. Are you going to come spy on me then?"

Next, she made him describe the white striations on her hips and across her lower back, above her ass. They looked like healed cuts from an X-Acto blade. Like rivers on a map.

"They started in my mid-twenties. Soon I'll be one big scar: a walking scar and bruise. Beautiful?"

"Yes," he said, and then felt sorry for saying it. He was often late detecting sarcasm. But as far as he knew, he'd meant it. If he were in a movie, and if he were a man wearing pants, he would trace her scars with his tongue.

"Show me something," she said.

"I have a pimple starting on my neck, right here," he said, cocking his head to one side.

"You don't have anything permanent, do you?"

A cold drop struck the crown of his head. It seemed to fall through his body and exit from the soles of his feet. He began to feel so cold he couldn't think about anything but his own skin. The woods were quiet. He couldn't put his wet shirt back on, so he crossed his arms and continued to shiver.

"I like your goose bumps," she said.

"Okay." He shivered.

"You don't have anywhere to go, do you?"

He shook his head.

"You can't stay here. You owe me a painting of a boot."

•

Her teapot whistled on the stove. She poured steaming water over a bag and the kitchen filled with the scent of spiced apple. Her rented cottage had a bench swing on the front porch and a garden plot in the backyard. Potted herbs grew in the windows of her art studio, a converted second bedroom. She set him up with an easel and supplies. She put her left bloodred boot on a sheet-covered stool.

"Have at it," she said.

Stephen heard the shower turn on. He started to sketch. It took him over two hours to accomplish a shitty underdrawing. He hadn't heard the shower turn off, but now he noticed it was no longer on. From the hallway, he could see Miss Baskin sleeping on her bed. He made some more tea. He removed the pot before it whistled. He added four spoons of sugar to his mug. It was so good. He was surprised; he'd never had tea before.

Sitting on a chair in Miss Baskin's room, he sipped his tea and watched her sleep. He brought in the easel and did a few quick paintings. He wasn't meticulous, like he'd been with the boot. He made thirteen. Miss Baskin tossed and turned, tangled up in the sheets. He painted her scars and veins, and then he left them there and got home too late for dinner. Ed was asleep with the TV on. Stephen fixed himself a plate and went up to his room to paint the other bloodred boot, the right one, late into the night.

•

Stephen carried an easel into the clearing and Miss Baskin carried two red umbrellas. She lay on her side, against the green moss, beneath one umbrella. Stephen tied the other umbrella to his easel, to protect his work from the tree eyes, which still trickled and splattered and would continue to weep for another month. Within a week, both umbrellas were lightly speckled with green.

He knew there was an unspoken agreement. Things would have to be even; he would paint her first, and then they would switch. They met on late afternoons and on weekends. They undressed in the graveyard and hid their clothes. They skipped school.

The first time he undressed in front of her, he had to close his eyes and face away from her while she painted him. The second time, two things happened. One, he got a boner. Two, he got embarrassed and cried just a little. She painted him anyway, as if nothing had happened. They both painted the whole figure first, and then they painted each other's individual parts in a progression. They made paintings of tear ducts, the backs of ears, napes, the undersides of breasts, nipples, elbows, navels, wrists, hip bones, assholes, the patch beneath his scrotum, her labia, his inner thigh, kneecaps and behind the knee, foot bottoms and tops. By the time they began working on toe tips and between the toes, the trees had run out of tears. The air in the wood turned bitter. Branches were skeletal and bare. The moss, which had grown to dangle from the red umbrellas in heavy cords, turned dark and stiff.

On the day the first snow fell, he was not surprised that she did not meet him in the graveyard. He didn't feel regret, but relief. The tree eyes began to close their lids for winter, but a few failed to shut, and those eyeballs hardened like marbles and grew crystals like old ice cream forgotten in the freezer.

•

Miss Baskin did not speak to Stephen beyond her brief, official interactions as teacher. He spent long hours in his bedroom, completing increasingly polished, more complicated versions of the paintings he'd started in the woods. Miss Baskin came over most evenings to eat salad at the round table. During grace one night, Ed described the glass windows of the new library, a project the town council had just awarded him. As before, Stephen examined Miss Baskin's face while Miss Baskin examined the intensely praying face of Ed, who told God about the electronic book stacks his company would install. They would open and close like accordions. Ed abruptly said amen, and then he asked Stephen about his very delinquent engagement present, as if it had occurred to him suddenly during his prayer.

Stephen fetched it from his room, where it had sat finished for over a month. Ed placed it on the mantel after dinner and all three of them gathered on the couch and looked.

Stephen met eyes with Miss Baskin, and in the silent language of looks that he knew from the woods, she signaled her approval without a smile, without moving her face at all.

"Terrific," said Ed. He clapped his hands together. He leaned over on the couch and awkwardly hugged his little brother. He asked Miss Baskin, "Where will we hang it?"

"I'll take it home," she said.

"No no no, it has to go someplace where people will see it. Like here," he said, holding it just above the fireplace mantle, where currently there hung a wreath of holly. "Or maybe…" he said, his voice turning soft, reverent. "In the library."

Stephen had wanted to impress Ed, but unveiling the painting felt weird, naked-weird, like he'd felt sometimes posing for Miss Baskin. Later, in the dark, he went to visit his parents in the graveyard. He couldn't help but feel sorry for them, couldn't help imagining how it must feel to stand still all night in the frozen air. It made death seem too long, too still. He had felt this for some time, which was why he kept a broom and a long-handled windshield scraper in the graveyard. He used to clean the ice and snow from his parents—and Uncle McCarty, too. He had an urge to wrap them in blankets or dress them in parkas. He had a compulsion to sweep and scrape clean the whole field of statues, to light fires between them, and to build them a roof. Thoughts like these, he knew, were why people like Ed were mayors and constructors of buildings, and he, Stephen, was not.

While he scraped his father free of ice, he saw a distant light in the woods. Snow and darkness obscured the frozen, labyrinthine creek, on which he kept slipping and falling. The light came from a small, strange campfire: Flames flicked out their tongues, and above them hovered colors and shapes that did not belong to fire. They looked like warped, watery movie projections.

Miss Mahogany crouched next to the fire and operated the library's newest, most expensive video camera. She waved him closer, and he crouched beside her. The flames came from a brazier of red-hot embers, onto which she tossed twigs, branches, and other small pieces of tree, bit by bit. Each piece burst into flame and released an image, recorded by the camera.

The first image was of one of Stephen's classmates, a girl named Charlie, who sat down on the moss and sliced red lines into her armpits with a razor blade. The stick burned up and the image faded. Some sticks did not yield a clear image. Some images consisted of a slow pan across empty woods, following something invisible. Other times, you could see one of Horusville's legions of masturbating children or hordes of adulterous adults, and plenty of wrinkled exhibitionist old folks from the retirement home too. The more branches she burned, the more the woods felt like a covert city parallel to the town in which he slept. He saw himself masturbating to *She-Hulk*, masturbating while gazing into the eyes of a tree, his math book beside him. He saw his own face up close, and it looked strangely sad and pained—which must be how the almond eyes saw him. He wished he hadn't seen it. It was the last thing he wanted anyone—even the almond eyes—to see. He felt like he was about to cry, but Miss Mahogany placed her hand on his shoulder. Then he saw himself with Miss Baskin, posing naked on the moss.

When Miss Mahogany's pile of sticks ran down, she doused the coals with snow and made Stephen lug her equipment back to the library, where she taught him to label and organize the recordings. Over the next several days, during study hall and after school, he helped her assign numbers, enter the new materials into the database, and store them in the chilly, humidity-controlled media room. He searched through years of database records for his parents' names, but when he located the files, the recordings were gone. He didn't ask her, but he suspected Miss Mahogany had predicted he'd look for them and had hidden them away. Once, he played footage of a man—someone he knew—having sex with his dog, who he also knew. Both were much older now than in the recording. Miss Mahogany sprinted across the room on her short stick legs and turned off the monitor.

"Hear me now, Sonny Jim!" she told him. "I've watched these all, and trust me when I tell you I'm battier now than I would've been. It's good information. But it's put me halfway to someplace else. You want to know how I do it? Do you?"

He shook his head no. She continued anyway.

"A mental tablet. A three-subject notebook of the mind. Every word goes on it before I speak it. Otherwise, all these images are coming out."

She tapped her finger on her forehead when she said this.

"That nasty man with his dog. Someone digging in the moss to bury God knows what. Huffers. Injectors. A full appendix to the *Kama Sutra*. It's not like I don't get a kick out of it, you know, but all of that in there…"

She pointed now to the media cabinets. She cradled her forehead in her hands and rocked it.

•

For the rest of the winter, Stephen recorded burning sticks in the woods and archived them in the library with Miss Mahogany. He sat in art class each day, too aware that he knew the skin beneath Miss Baskin's breasts. He stayed up late in his bedroom to paint what he knew of her. When they made eye contact, he was startled to recall in rapid succession the concentric designs of her iris, thumbprint, anus, navel, and heels. Sometimes she drew caricatures of students on their birthdays, but Stephen's passed with a blank chalkboard. It hurt. But he thought he understood why she couldn't make a cartoon of him. It had to do with her breath on his leg when she came in close to paint him. There was nothing left to say, or draw. Winter filled the woods with ice and snow. Stephen felt thankful for his work in the archives; otherwise, he'd have nowhere to go.

Then the weather changed, and the freezer-burned eyes shed their crystals. Sockets crackled and quivered, and lids unstuck with a faint snap. Ice dripped from branches, and the forest floor shifted from white to green. The eyes darted wildly about, learning how to see again. When the moss finally softened into a deep sponge, and the air smelled like earth, and the eyes resumed their creepy scanning, Stephen saw Miss Baskin naked in the woods again. Ed was naked, too. They had a bottle of champagne, and they danced naked and drank from the bottle. They had a picnic basket. Miss Baskin started a painting of Ed, and Stephen thought he knew just how she'd progress, how she would paint him piece by piece. But five minutes into the painting, before she'd finished even one piece, Ed got impatient, tackled her onto the moss, and they fucked. Stephen wanted to look away, but he didn't. The worst was their faces, the way they didn't look sad at all.

He remembered how ridiculous he'd looked in the recorded image, masturbating to the almond-eyed tree, and how pathetic he'd looked, letting Miss Baskin come in close to paint every part of him. It was painful to think of Miss Baskin and Ed, in this place—in the woods he'd always thought of as his—fucking every day while the trees recorded it. He felt strange enough, sad enough, to go home in search of a hatchet. He didn't even know if they had a hatchet at home, so instead he fetched the long-handled windshield scraper from the graveyard.

Ed and Miss Baskin lay on the moss together until sunset, and Stephen watched them until they left. Then he stared for a long time into the glade's largest eye, embedded in a trunk and big as a hubcap. He studied his own reflection in its wet surface. He struck it once in the middle with the scraper, catching the lid half open. He hacked at it, all around it. Bark chipped away, chunking off the tree's white meat. The slick of pupil oozed down the trunk. He chopped the glade blind. Inside each eye was a rope of snot followed by a gob of red. It stained the bark and his skin. He plucked the eyes that dangled off limbs. They quivered in his hands. He lined up the trembling eyes on the moss.

He stabbed the first plucked eye and couldn't stop stabbing until he dug through the moss with the scraper, digging deep, more than a foot, until he finally reached dirt. There were still more eyes he'd not blinded—eyes too high on trunks and branches, eyes throughout the forest, and he'd never blind them all. They'd remember and record what he'd just done, which was worse than the masturbating, worse than his brother's fucking, maybe even worse than the man who'd fucked his dog. Whatever his parents had done, whatever their hidden tapes revealed, he knew the file in the archive with his name would now be worse. He cried, and the eye blood swirled with his own tears and snot. He was glad his parents were dead and couldn't see him. No one, he felt, deserved to be seen like this.

He tossed the still-quivering eyes into the creek, now rushing with snowmelt. Every kid in Horusville who'd ever plucked an eye was aware that the eyes could look around in a mason jar of water for at least a week before wilting and going black. He watched them bob and twist away, and he wondered if the trees would chronicle these travels.

The recordings, Stephen felt strongly now, belonged to the recorded, who deserved to know that their secrets were not secret. Maybe some of them even deserved to see who they really were. After dark, he pushed wheelbarrow loads of media material through the streets of Horusville, following the same route he'd bicycled every morning for years when he was a paperboy. He set the recordings in stacks on each porch. Just after midnight, he crawled into bed and, shortly thereafter, someone set the woods on fire.

Stephen found Miss Mahogany at the head of the crowd, with her video camera, filming the images that flickered into the sky. The volunteer fire squad worked to keep the blaze from skipping onto rooftops, and the populace of Horusville set up lawn chairs as if it were a Fourth of July display. Soon enough, mothers covered their children's eyes. Some people went home and retched, unable to stomach the small-scale history of Horusville that hovered above the woods, against the screen of night sky. Most watched. Stephen gently pulled the camera from Miss Mahogany's hands and tossed the camera into the fire, where the contents of the media cabinets already sizzled and hissed. Last of all, the trees shot up the image of everyone there, in real time, eyes and mouths dumbly open.

LOST IN THE FOREST OF MECHANICAL BIRDS

THE MECHANIC'S THIRTEEN-YEAR-OLD SON sat alone in the deep snow in the middle of a burnt wood of black trees, on the verge of freezing to death. The farmhouse was now a burned box, the barn workshop a smoldering rectangle. There was nowhere to go and no one left to come get him. He predicted he would soon fall asleep and not wake up again, but this was not what scared him: he had reason to suspect that, in place of blood and guts, his insides were makeshift clockwork, fashioned by his father from broken appliance pieces and other odd parts. Perhaps it was insanity brought on by the cold, or by what he had done—but if it were true, he would not drift into sleep and dream and die; he would remain like he was, shivering and solitary in the forest of charred trunks and branches. To test this idea, he'd several times taken his .22 handgun, a Christmas present from his father, and pushed the barrel into his stomach with the intention of pulling the trigger, but he didn't really want to, and anyway, there was still time for sleep to take him. He began to cry.

•

The morning of Christmas Eve, the same as any morning, he'd lifted himself off the hearthrug to sift through the night's ashes for coals to start the day's fire. His mother was a snoring lump beneath a pile of blankets on the sofa. His father was gone—a thin blan-

ket folded into a neat square on the cushion of the reading chair
where he slept. The son again heard the sound that had woken
him, the clang of metal hitting metal, and only now was he sure it
hadn't come from a dream but from the mechanic's workshop in
the barn. He flipped through the pages of the mechanic's drafting
pad. It began with realistic sketches of various birds. Then a claw
was replaced by a bent dinner fork, and a skeletal construction of
wire formed an outstretched wing. Complex systems of pulleys
connected beak, wing, and tail. Details of an inner eye revealed the
interlocking teeth of tiny gears, which spun to dilate a pupil. For
the rest of the day, curled up in front of the fire, his father's distant
clanking in the background, he turned the pages of his tattered
book and read yet again the tale of two knights, brothers, each
tricked into giving up his heraldic coat of arms for an unmarked
shield; in this way the brothers met again as strangers and fought
for an entire day, neither of them realizing the mistake until each
had fatally wounded the other.

Late Christmas Eve, when his mother was knitting and they
were watching the final log of the evening catch fire, the mechanic entered loudly in his work boots and set on the mantelpiece a
heavy object draped with an oily rag. There was a loud whir, which
the son clearly recognized as the blender his mother had used in
the days before the mechanic quit all other things and took to
watching birds. It began to wobble and shake.

•

The sound of the blender reminded the son that things had once
been otherwise—they hadn't always lived in the den. In what
seemed like pictures from a dream or past life, he remembered the
other rooms of the house when they were kept warm and well-lit.
The last time he'd seen his own room, all the old toys and even the
walls were encrusted in ice, and a frozen, slippery waterfall gushed
from a busted pipe in the wall as though trapped in time, forever

cascading down the once-creaky stairs his father had carried him
up to bed.

He didn't remember exactly when his father had decided to do
nothing but sit at the picture window with long black binoculars
and watch for birds, none of which had returned since the woods
had burned, with the exception of the barn owl that scratched
around in the workshop rafters. In the evenings, one could sometimes catch the flicker of white wings swooping through black
trees. Because there were no other birds, the dated sightings beside
"barn owl" in his father's field guide ran several columns long.

He wasn't sure if it was before or after his father's birdwatching
and the slow growth of ice on the walls that his mother had begun
breaking all the household appliances. Over time she broke nearly
all they had, but he remembered the blender best—not just because it proved very difficult to break, but because his mother had
broken it with such determined ferocity, her face contorted and
ugly while she held it overhead and flung it again and again at the
kitchen floor. At the time, he'd been reading a story about a sorcer-
ess who'd conspired to trap a sorcerer in the trunk of a tree. His
mother's face, which had seemed about to snap, somehow contorted further each time she turned on the blender and listened to the
blades continue to whir with seamless perfection. It was an older
blender, nearly an antique, made when things were put together
well and with good parts. The mechanic himself had reconditioned
the motor, cleaned and lubricated every internal crevice, and presented it as a gift. In a shower of sparks, and with several two-
handed whacks from a chef's knife, his mother chopped through
the cord, and the whirring stopped. She then turned the blender
over to her son, who, as he'd been directed with all the other broken things, brought it to his father, who, as each time before, did
not remove his eyes from whatever blackened, birdless limb his
lenses magnified. The son set the blender on the pile of junk that
had grown around his father and went back to reading his story.

When the cold air glazed the big picture window and frosted the lenses of the binoculars, all three gathered in the den, where the fire warmed them. For a short while things were better. His mother's face was not contorted with anger, and there were no appliances to break. He could see his father's eyes, which blinked with boredom. His mother's stare was also blank, directionless. Still, it was better. Then his father began to scribble on the drafting pad, and the nub of graphite whispered across the paper. Keeping his eyes close to the paper, the mechanic was absent again. As if in response to this, his mother began knitting, and she knitted so her needles clacked together intolerably, and even while she slept, her grinding teeth clacked as if she were furiously knitting together her own dreams. All of this noise gave him a headache that persisted so long that by Christmas Eve he'd forgotten he had a headache until the whir of the blender motor brought it to an entirely new crescendo.

•

The object continued to shake on the mantelpiece, then steadied itself by pressing two glinting claws deep into the wood. Two wings stretched out, flapped twice, and the bird glided noisily to perch on the backrest of the mechanic's reading chair. It somewhat resembled the tiny winter wrens that, in the years before the wood caught fire, would settle on the slender twigs of the farmhouse bushes. But the mechanic's wren was over three feet tall and composed of motley metals. It perched silently and motionlessly for a short time, and then the whirring began again. The son covered his head with his book, and his mother stood up, prepared to defend her home with knitting needles. The whirring preceded a jerky cock of the head, an avian flick of the eyelids, and then the beak opened, emitting two rings, clearly the bell from the mechanic's antique bicycle. Mother and son laughed nervously, and the father could not conceal a proud smile.

Unlike a real wren, which is in constant, jittery motion, the mechanical wren was largely still and silent. Occasionally it shocked the room with a loud whir, adjusting its feet on the perch or slowly flapping one wing to maintain balance. It was a wren in shape only; neither symmetrical nor uniform, the bird was a patchwork of sprockets, springs, bolts, nuts, wire, and hammer-flattened metal from hubcaps and baking sheets. The mother's steam iron was partially discernible, and the son observed the ball-bearing ring from a roller-skate wheel. A spark plug jutted out of the dimpled chrome breast at an angle. Although distinctly birdlike, the form was crude enough to be also vaguely manlike, a homunculus of appliances and spare parts.

Several hours later, they'd become more accustomed to the sound of the blender motor. Curled up on the hearthrug, the son kept a watchful eye on the wren, its various metals glimmering faintly in the firelight. The middle-of-the-night whirrings warranted only a half-opened eyelid. Then a final whir, barely distracting the family from sleep, was followed by a shattered windowpane and a bitter gust of air. The mechanical wren blended into the black rectangle of night. They rushed to block out the icy wind by stapling layers of blankets to the window frame. They swept up the broken glass.

Because it was close enough to Christmas, they decided to exchange gifts. In addition to a blanket, the mother had been knitting dark blue mittens and a dark blue hat with earflaps. The son put them on and took from between the pages of his book a sheaf of paper onto which he'd rewritten a ballad, replacing the characters with his parents and revising some of the details. The mother gave the blanket to the mechanic, who, when he was done admiring it, folded it into a neat square and placed it on his chair. The mechanic then presented a .22 target pistol in one hand and a tiny sculpture of wire in the other. He whimsically crisscrossed his hands, extending gun to mother, sculpture to son. It was a tiny owl, with a ring so it could be worn as a pendant.

"It's a joke," said the mechanic, and he switched the gifts to the rightful recipients. The mother removed a gold cross from her necklace and fastened the owl. The son, sitting cross-legged in front of the fire, rested the gun on his lap. He had shot at cans with a pellet gun before, but this pistol was altogether darker and oilier. He put a finger on the trigger and was eager to squeeze, but didn't.

"It's not a full-grown gun," said his father with some amusement. "But you'll grow into it." That night they all lay awake in the dark, shivering.

When the son woke the next morning, his father had already left for the workshop, and he did not return that night, or any other night, to sleep. The new blanket remained folded on the chair. The son kept close watch on their supply of kindling and logs, and whenever it ran low, he pulled his red wagon up to the barn, where rows of firewood were stacked against an outside wall, kept dry under tarps. Although he was curious about the nature of his father's work, he did not have the courage to knock on the big barn door. He'd return from these trips with a teetering wagonload of wood to tell his mother about the barn owl's white, spectral swoop through twilight. He did not tell her that the woods had begun to fill with mechanical birds.

•

The burnt trees made simple, arterial shapes against the gray sky. The fire had shorn away all twigs and lesser branches, and some trees had the molten look of black metal sculptures. Absent underbrush and leaves, the uncluttered expanse of snow was clean and open. He liked this better: a snowfield of warped obelisks, as opposed to the more tangled and unruly version of nature. And yet he couldn't like it blamelessly, since he'd been author of the fire. It seemed so long ago that he had taken a rake through a burning pile of autumn leaves to expose the untouched layers beneath the ash; a single, papery leaf

had risen on an invisible wave of heat, caught fire in the air, and with
the jerky flits of a bat, followed the tunnel of smoke into the woods.
There had been nothing to do but let it eat its way through the trees,
leaving behind a field of clean black bones.

The frozen, waterless air focused everything into clear detail.
When he stood still and aimed his .22 at an imagined target, he
could hear silence behind his breath and heartbeat. The snow was
crunchy on top, powder beneath, so the initial resistance to each
step gave way to a deep, feathery drop. Each step made a loud,
squeaky racket that seemed to emanate from within his head. He
paused every so often to aim at an empty branch.

He squeaked along awkwardly in this way until he felt he was
more or less in the middle of the wood. He knew from experience
that the wood had many middles; once you got so far in, any place
you chose to stand felt like it must be the center of something.
He paused again to aim at what he expected would be an empty
branch. Startled, he pivoted in a circle. Mechanical birds sat stoi-
cally in the branches. He was afraid, but his fear was not the same
as if, for example, he had startled a bear, not the expected, rational,
immediate fear of being mauled and eaten. It was what someone
might have felt in the same wood two hundred years before, stum-
bling upon the carved faces of a lone totem pole in the middle of
nowhere. An abrupt, anachronistic encounter with a human mind
in the wilderness. The sudden loss of feeling alone.

They perched like statues. He did not know if their stillness
was by design (a response to his clumsy approach) or lack of design
(maybe they were broken). The crudest bird stood out to him; he
aimed at the wren fashioned from the blender. He squeezed. The
bullet clanged. The wren tottered and fell, not unlike a soda can
skimmed by a BB. Inspired, he took aim at the most frighten-
ing one, which had two giant rasp files for a bill and fork tines
that formed a crest on its head. Before he was ready to shoot, he
sensed a faint electric hum. It became a buzz, which turned into a

cacophony of whirling and spinning gears as the entire flock took flight at once. The wren, lying heavily on its back in the deep snow, struggled to spread its wings. He smashed it with the pistol butt until the blender ground to a halt.

He carried the wren by its welded feet. He was hungry and thought of his mother, back at the farmhouse, warming chicken bouillon and the last egg over the fire. He tossed the metal against the large barn door with a reverberating thump. The mechanic didn't open. He brought a wagonload of firewood down to the house, then sat in front of the fire with his soup to read about an evil knight who dangled the slain bodies of good knights from the limbs of a tree.

Each day he went out to kill what his father had made and thumped it against the barn door. Each day he discovered a new bird perched on a black limb among the flock. He was sure he could kill faster than his father could create.

He killed a colorful thumb-sized hummingbird that repeatedly landed on his barrel and obstructed his aim, wings buzzing like an electric razor. Bejeweled with sequins and rhinestones, costume rubies for eyes, it was like an ornamental egg confected by a jeweler. Something within its intricate clockwork tinkled like miniature wind chimes. It looked like a gift. He smacked it with a volley of rocks, and it flitted in tight, paranoid circles close to the ground. He crushed it under the heel of his boot and flung it against the barn door.

The next time he entered the woods, black wings grazed his head. A razored beak snipped his cheek. Blood drops hit the snow and bloomed through the crystals. The new, shadowlike bird disappeared before he could see it clearly.

Each bird the son destroyed was replaced by a shadow-bird. They were the simplest in design, like skeletal crows. The body of each was a black coil from an automobile suspension. Within the coiled ribcage, the guts spun in a quiet but constant blur. A large black hex nut made a head, and the hex-shaped hole an eye. Welded to each head was a sharp beak: a rusted ice pick, the blade of a pocketknife, half a pair of scissors or pruning shears. The dark wings were edged with sharpened metal. Pronged feet made of nails. They gouged the back of his neck and slit the top of his ear. He threw himself flat into the snow at every moving shadow.

The few times he managed to hit one, the bullet ricocheted off. They dove at him in groups, and he ran from the wood, his knitted hat torn, scalp cut, hair tangled with dry blood. He took to running through the wood with leather gloves, a thick jacket, safety glasses, and a slightly small football helmet. He spun in berserk circles with his pistol and swatted at his helmet while they swooped over him. Beneath each tail (a feathered fan of kitchen knives), he could see a wind-up key, the type used to propel an old toy, or to spin the dancer on a music box, or to rejuvenate the pendulum of a grandfather clock. Slowly, the keys turned.

•

After Christmas, his mother resumed her knitting. She took back the mechanic's blanket and began to knit everything she'd ever made into a much, much larger blanket that soon resembled less a blanket than a ragged sail with dangling mitten fingers, parts of hats, bits of scarves, and slipper heels. Within this sail-blanket, he could see his own cut-up hat and mittens, with their spots of dried blood visible as small pieces of the patchwork. She seemed always tired and couldn't clack her needles, so instead of this noise, she had developed a long, wheezing foghorn of a cough. Too afraid to leave the house after the flock of shadow-birds had pecked him so violently, he'd let the fire burn low to conserve wood. Slowly, the ice had begun to crackle, vein-like, along the walls, and his mother's coughed-up breath took ghostly shape in the air. When the last log had smoldered down to embers, his mother ran out of wool. She faintly wheezed something about the cold, then, instead of using her motley blanket to sail away her sofa as he'd imagined, she rolled herself up into her knitting, a cocoon, and slept silently and ceased to cough or even grind her teeth. It took him two days to work up the courage to poke her ashen cheek with his finger. Even after he cupped his hands together and warmed her skin with his breath, she still felt like stone.

The silence, except for the crackling veins of ice, grew to be too much. He more dragged than rolled his red wagon through the deep snow up to the barn, the too-small helmet giving him a headache. From the barn roof, a dark row of hex-shaped heads stared at him with vacant hex-shaped holes of gray sky. Without even bothering to aim his gun, he flipped over the wagon and scrambled under it as best he could, waiting for the rap of sharp beaks. It didn't come. They were diving at the field on the other side of the barn.

In the field, the barn owl fluttered its wings in bursts and hopped several feet at a time while the shadow-crows casually swooped down to cut it. Some perched heavily on the owl until it managed to flap them off. There was a trail of white feathers, spotted with black marks of blood. The owl cried. The son held a shadow-crow in his gunsight while it pecked at the dying bird with what he recognized as the corkscrew from his camping knife. He fired. The crow flapped away. The owl flailed, losing feathers. He flipped the owl over and put the barrel to its forehead. The eyelids blinked. His shot echoed off the barn. The hex-shaped holes stared emptily.

He built a giant fire in the field, and it melted a wide circle of snow. It was dark. His bonfire illuminated the side of the barn and part of the roof. At the very edge of the light, barely visible, the crows perched. When he let the fire burn lower, they hopped forward. When he added wood, they retreated back into the shadow. A clunk above startled him. A crow rolled down the roof, slid off the edge, and plopped into the snow. Each hour the crows expired in increasing numbers.

He butchered the owl with the pruning-shear beak of a defunct crow. He held the lukewarm heart in his mouth, thinking himself like a reverent indigenous hunter, but then he spat out the heart without chewing and placed it in the snow. He made a pile of the white feathers. He made groupings of bones, beak, feet. He even kept what blood he could, letting it pool in the basin of his upturned helmet. Two-thirds of the meat he set aside in the snow for his mother's soup, even though he knew there would be no waking her to eat it. The rest he roasted over the fire and ate slowly, piece by piece, letting the juices float throughout his mouth.

He doused the fire with snow, except for a single torch that he walked down to the farmhouse and touched to his mother's knitted shroud. When he saw flames lick the eaves of the house roof he was satisfied and went to the barn. He stacked the rest of the firewood against the big door, lit it, and fanned the forked tongues until they surged overhead. Then he stepped back ten careful paces, widened his stance, and aimed the gun.

•

Alone in the deep snow in the middle of the burnt wood of black trees, he'd stopped crying. He felt so numb that he imagined he was without a body. He drifted into sleep, remembering how good it had been to hold each thin slice of owl on his tongue until it was cool, until he could no longer tell it was there, and then to swallow with what had been his first sincerely spiritual sentiment. In his dreams, he repeated the ritual again and again: He shot the owl, butchered it, piece by piece filled himself with its spirit, burned his dead mother, and set the barn ablaze. He fired the gun three times into his father, eyes wide, hair and clothes on fire, and walked into the woods as far as he could before his internal clockwork seized in the cold and he had to sit down, curl up onto his side, and dream and dream again.

THE BABYCATCHER

THE MIDDLE-AGED COUPLE DROVE from the suburbs of their mid-western city—maybe Dayton, Indianapolis, or Detroit (it barely matters which one; so many couples from so many Mid-American cities had made the same drive)—to meet the man called the Baby-catcher. They were desperate. They'd tried in vitro twice. Three adoptions had fallen through. They still had that hungry look in their eyes when they gazed upon other people's infants—that voracious stare that made new parents smile at first, then frown, then clutch their swaddled bundles as they hurried away.

They'd been given directions by the Doula. She was one of those super high-end birth coaches who had the exact right pedigree to come up through the doula ranks and break into the wealthier suburbs—both a nursing background and time spent holding workshops in yoga centers and spirituality bookstores, dreadlocked, the whiff of patchouli. She charged top dollar. There was a rumor—had to be apocryphal, someone's joke—that she'd once orchestrated a birth in a river, during which the mom-to-be held tight with both hands to a rope strung across a quick channel, letting the baby flow from her like a fish into the current, to be caught by the father with a net downstream. There were lots of stories like this about the Doula. She was a legend.

But the Doula had lost her own baby in childbirth and left town. When the ravenous couple spotted her, it was at a farmer's market an hour away, where they'd gone to avoid the usual friends, the usual questions. It must've been the same for the Doula. But how was it she now had a perfect angel suckling at her breast, when she'd lost her own not months before? When the Doula saw the couple, she all but ran from them. They chased her down.

"How?" they asked.

"I don't recommend it," she said.

"We have to know," they said. The hunger-desire gleaming in their eyes brought to mind that poem about goblin men selling goblin fruit.

"Some call him the Babycatcher."

•

The directions were nearly impossible. They exited one of those rural, interstate off-ramps that features only the hollowed shell of a long-defunct gas station. Then they drove roads with no painted lines and no names— just numbers and cardinal directions (like East 700 South) that make little sense to suburban people. Then lanes with no signs at all, just covered bridges and barns to serve as landmarks. Then a gravel road, missing much of its gravel. They cut the chain across the road with bolt cutters, just like the Doula had told them they must. After passing it once, they reversed and found the lane—more of a path—disguised by brush. They hauled branches aside. The bumper of their SUV mowed down little saplings while they drive slowly through deep ruts. A few miles like this, and then they found him.

The Babycatcher (not what he calls himself; he doesn't tell such couples what he calls himself) wore a leather vest with no shirt beneath it. His black hat sported a colorful feather. He was an extremely fit-looking man, if a hair too skinny. A handsome, chiseled, angular face, cheeks slightly hollowed. Seldom without a piece of grass or straw clenched between his teeth. The strip of hair running from between his chest muscles down into his rough-leather pants was both sexy and repellant, alluring and indecent.

He leaned against a corral fence, chewing his reed, while they approached him.

"Perhaps you are wanting one of these," he said with a slightly rolled *r*, accent hard to place.

(He never referred to them as babies—was very careful not to call them anything at all).

The Babycatcher spoke like a man with supply and demand very much on his side. You wanted. He had. You were desperate. He was content. Any exchange would be in his favor. That was the beginning and end of it.

Later, they would vaguely remember a falling-down barn or two. Maybe a paint-flaking farmhouse. Maybe equipment, maybe a tractor. It was hard to see such things because the whole place smelled delicious—like fresh-baked bread and pastries and sugar cookies—a scent that can only come from a baby head, from the little things running circles in the man's corral: adorable cherubs with the plumpest legs, with so many wrinkles. Around and around they went, in a kind of pack, laughing and giggling.

Beyond the corral, on a wagon (maybe hitched to a tractor, it was hard to remember) were stacked cages of lashed-together sticks or bones, and within these containers were more of the sweet little things sitting on their fat bums, eyes bright with tears. Several of them were wailing. The wife couldn't take her eyes off them. The Babycatcher noticed.

"No, no, no. You don't want those," he told her. "They aren't broken yet. It is one of these you want." He gestured at the corral.

She couldn't take her eyes off the crying ones. She imagined rocking each in her arms, saying "Shh, shh, shh," until they fell asleep, one by one.

"These ones are ready," he said, nodding to the corral. "Those," he said, nodding to the cages, "are fresh and wild from the woods."

The husband knew what to do. The whole world had disappeared to his wife, except the babies on that wagon. "How much?" The Babycatcher laughed. The husband did not.

"Really, no joke?" the bare-chested man finally said. The husband noticed the man's accent thickening just a little.

Maybe the Babycatcher was surprised. Maybe this wasn't part of his sales pitch. Maybe the couple's category of desperate was at a level even he rarely saw. But probably not. This was probably how it usually went.

The Babycatcher let out a long, low whistle. "The little ones you look at are spoken for. Your wife thinks she can only be happy with one pulled from the trees." He shook his head. "I don't recommend it." He shrugged.

The husband's whisper was barely audible. "Please," he said.

The Babycatcher made a slight movement, just a twitch, and the ugliest dog anyone ever saw came bounding up behind him. It had black gums and black teeth and was nearly hairless except for patches of stiff bristles, and with strange extra nipples on its side, back, and rump. The mammary glands dribbled yellow milk.

"She's ugly, yes?" he said. "It wasn't my plan to go back this season. They are changing their patterns, beginning their migrations to hibernate. But if there is a wild pack of them out there still. Really bright ones. Really…" He seemed to be searching for a word. "…*fresh*. If they are still there then *this*, my beautiful, ugly sniffer beast, will find them." The Babycatcher looked up at the sky and squinted. "It's not too late, maybe? For a price."

"Anything," the husband said. From his jacket, he pulled out a little notebook and uncapped a pen. "Jot down your price."

The Babycatcher took the writing implements and, holding the pen like a farmer holds his fork, scratched down barely legible numbers.

The husband laughed. "There are an extra two zeroes."

The Babycatcher looked at it again. Squinted. Counted the zeroes out loud. Shook his head to say no, those zeroes were correct.

"But that…that's a mortgage."

"This is correct," said the Babycatcher. "A trip to the woods this late in the season, for the wildest, freshest ones you've ever seen. You can take your pick. This is the first time I've offered this to anyone."

The wife, who'd been fixated on the cages, shook with a startle, as if waking from a dream.

The couple glanced at each other. She made a face that told the husband it would be okay, they didn't have to ruin themselves financially—not for happiness. They could live unhappily but comfortably. She touched his shoulder as she stared at the weeping babies. He would clearly spend twice as much to avoid whatever misery he imagined, whatever unhappiness his mind was conjuring that he couldn't see. In other words, they made the decision together. It wasn't her, wasn't him. The combination of them—and the fact that they loved each other more than anything—is what did it. They say love conquers all, but the couple had no idea what *all* would end up including. And when was conquering ever a good thing?

The couple nodded in agreement. They discussed the fine details with the leather-vested man. It would have to be before the weather turned, at which time they (he was careful to never call them babies) went deeper into the woods, into the burrows and hollow trees where they wintered, where even the Babycatcher (not what he called himself) couldn't fish them out. And jewels: he was a man who would only be paid in metals and gems, with a note of appraisal. That was the deal. He told them how they would need to dress—not like they were now, but for the deep forest. And he told them what to bring in their bags.

•

The car was sold. The second mortgage was obtained through a friend of a friend who rushed it for them, as people can do in the wealthier suburbs. Money was borrowed from an aging parent, with the promise to pay it back. The details might be boring, but the gathering of money—searching gem dealers, gold dealers—was a full-time job. They barely slept. They liquidated. They bought gold. They bought diamonds. The people they dealt with looked more acceptable than the Babycatcher, but there was also something similarly criminal about them, except without the man's confusing sexiness.

They followed the directions he'd given them. They took a similar, rural interstate exit, but this time there was no defunct gas station, just tall weeds. They drove numbered and then not-numbered backroads. They unfastened the chain, which was unlocked this time, just as the man had promised. Although how could the same road be here, after driving in an altogether different direction? Probably all gravel paths look the same.

Forty-five minutes of bumpy driving and there he was, waiting for them. He had no vehicle. He still wore his leather vest with no shirt beneath it, his black hat with a feather, a fresh little twig between his teeth.

He inspected the gems and gold with a loupe he took from a pouch he wore on his belt. A giant backpack rested against a nearby tree, with nets and traps hanging off every which way. Plus a crossbow.

"Surely, there's no need for something like that," said the husband.

The Babycatcher half-smiled, half-sneered. He pocketed his payment. He made a small motion, and his hideous, long-snouted, bristle-haired, mammary-mottled mutt bounded out of the woods, paused, dripping yellowed milk onto the leaves, snorted, and then bounded back into the woods. "This way," the man said.

There wasn't really a hiking path—just a series of game trails that would fade in and out of existence. They walked an hour into the woods like this, the couple struggling to keep pace.

"I told you not to wash," the man said. He sniffed each of them.

"We didn't. We haven't washed since we saw you."

"The stink of the world is still on you." He gave them a bottle of something. Made them squirt out droplets, rub it on their skin. "Rub it all over," he said. He motioned to their underarms, their crotches, their feet. "All over."

At first the liquid smelled like death and decay, but that soon faded and it only smelled earthy, like rotting leaves, mushrooms, soil.

"Here," said the Babycatcher a short while later. He crouched near a trail like all the other game trails they'd seen, inspecting something that was invisible to the couple. He summoned the balding, dripping dog. He gave it an order in a language the couple couldn't understand. It didn't seem to want to obey, whining, snarling. The man said his command in a harsher, almost violent tone, and the dog slunk away through the trees, back the way they'd come. "It would eat too many of them," he explained with a shrug and a smile.

The Babycatcher set his nets. His snares. A series of them. Then he arranged the biggest one, which he carefully hid just off the trail. This one he could work with a pulley from up in a tree.

He put on spiked boots to climb into the canopy to rig his contraption. He descended partway down the tree and motioned for them to join him, and they all waited up in the branches, in extreme discomfort, backs and asses aching. The Babycatcher chewed his twig and held on to a thin rope, not much more than a string, which disappeared up into the canopy, likely connected to the pulleys and rigs and tackle that worked the biggest net down below. Watching him rig it so high up on thin limbs was like gawking at high-wire acrobatics with no safety net. Maybe that's just what it took. Maybe it was a kind of show he put on to make them feel like he'd risked his neck to earn their fee.

They were crepuscular things. At dusk they came running down the trail. Just three at first. The Babycatcher knew they were coming. He clamped a hand over the wife's mouth, correctly anticipating that she would gasp.

The beauty of them! Oh, perfect naked cherubs running down the trail through the trees! Their bare, fat little legs moving in such a way that it looked like they would fall and tumble. The husband reached out both arms from his perch, mentally trying to catch one should it fall. Their faces bright, eyes almost glowing with happiness! They were running fast along a rough trail, at an age when surely no regular baby could do that. The couple didn't think about it. Later, they wouldn't be able to remember if the woods had been filled with bright giggling, or if it was the jolly way they moved that made the human heart hear peals of baby-laughter in the silence.

The three little ones quickly disappeared into the flora. Before the couple could open their mouths, the man put his fingers to his lips. Not a minute later, the three came back. They gathered around one snare after another, poking them with little sticks, springing each trap except for the big one. They smiled gummy, toothless smiles. Some of them had hair, some were bald. All had deep dimples in their butts that made you need to pinch them. You wanted your fingers tickling them, you wanted to kiss their every chubby fold. You wanted to love and be so loved. The three ran back down the trail, going back the way they'd originally come.

The Babycatcher gave the couple a look as if to say *Here they come.*

A herd of babies came tumbling down the trail now. The giggles! The toothless gums! The dimples! There must've been fifty of them. When the path was dense and overflowing with chubby legs and bellies, the Babycatcher sprang his big net, lifting seven of them high into the air. How they cried, how they squealed! The rest of them gathered right beneath the trap, reaching up with pudgy arms and the tiniest fingers, eyes suddenly dripping tears. They screamed their little hearts out. For hours they did this, like the worst late-night colic you've ever seen. Babies above screaming, babies below screaming.

"Can't we do something?" husband and wife whispered, clutching each other.

The man twirled a weighted knife in his fingers and looked down with cold eyes that quieted the couple. There was something to it. What would happen if you descended the tree into that pack? The way the Babycatcher spun his blade and shifted on his perch told the couple the cherubs below weren't as defenseless as one might think.

Only when darkness deepened did the things on the ground run down the trail again to wherever they made their nightly nest. Who knows what kind of predators might hunt them in a forest like this? The Babycatcher descended the tree, waved the couple down the trunk after him. They hauled the net back through the woods by the faint yellow beam of a light affixed to the man's forehead. By the time they got through to where they'd parked their car, the chubby, sobbing things were shit-smeared but still beautiful.

"Take your pick," said the Babycatcher. For half an hour he was quiet, patient while they deliberated. "I don't have all night," he finally said. "Most know which one at first sight."

It was true. They did. The one they chose—their baby, as they already thought of it—was the same one they'd both set their hearts on from the moment they'd seen it lifted from the trail hours ago. They'd already raised it up a thousand times in their minds. It had already visited at Christmas in their old age, with grandchildren in tow.

They strapped it into the car seat. They'd come prepared, they had all the equipment ready. They mixed a bottle of formula and evenly heated it in a bottle warmer plugged into the SUV's USB drive. She sat in back while he drove. She fed it warm milk. It gulped. It slept. You could say it slept like a baby.

•

How to describe those weeks of happiness? The relief? They were tired. It ate constantly. Not only that, but it ran fast and nimble—at an age that should've raised eyebrows. They were happy, they told themselves, but also stressed. They were in a pickle. How to unveil a child that they didn't have before to friends, family, and coworkers? You can't stroll an infant that looks, say, nine to twelve months old already—and not just walking but running, running fast—down a block as if nothing has happened. How to say where they'd gotten it? They emailed the Doula to ask: What does one do—what are the next steps? She did not reply. The email bounced back. Her social media accounts and all those tens of thousands of followers she'd carefully curated over the years had vanished. She had changed one life for another. That must be the only way.

In any case, they had to sell the house. They'd been too optimistic about how to make ends meet after paying the Babycatcher's fee, liquidating their retirement accounts, financing the second mortgage. They'd been too swept up in just getting to their goal of a baby, thinking that would be the end of it all. Now, it cried all night—a kind of cry that told them it missed its pack, missed its forest. In their new, rented, more affordable house there was no sleeping, no way to clearly crunch numbers and make things work. Parental leave wasn't on the table. There was no doctor to sign the papers. She quit her job. He got a negative review at work. How to explain it all to someone on the outside, what their world had become?

The baby did not calm, did not acclimate. It did not grow. It bit them. It learned to open the doors—to unlock them—and would run out in the middle of the night. The husband once had to tackle it, and twisted his ankle, limped for weeks rather than see a doctor. They bought salvaged fencing with money they didn't have and fenced their rented backyard. The baby gnawed on the wood posts. They found it eating a still-warm bird, gumming the still-warm heart of a mouse.

They didn't regret it. The baby was theirs. Their happiness, their very own problem of their very own making. They still loved their problem with all their hearts. "Why did we need a wild one?" they whispered at night, between bouts of colic. "We should have let him train it"—they couldn't say *break*, as he had—"in his corral."

"Will he help us?"

"He'll train it."

"Yes, all that gold."

"Yes, all those jewels."

But how to find your way back to the Babycatcher? They drove down rural lanes, to dirt lanes, looking for his barn and corrals. They followed the directions they'd written down from the Doula—who they couldn't find anywhere now, not through old web pages, not through old social media pages gone inactive. Direct message after direct message unanswered. Then, the old pages disappeared, and they had to make a whole new account to see that they'd been blocked.

They woke to find the baby high in a tree branch, dismembering a squirrels' nest. They found stray piles of guts on the doormat, on the kitchen floor, like a cat would leave. The thing left steaming innards at the foot of their bed, a whole pile—several cats', several dogs', several something's worth.

As the piles of guts increased, the pets in the neighborhood decreased. Missing posters were tacked to telephone poles. It was becoming uncomfortable, the way their child looked at neighborhood children from the window. It wanted to play. This worried them deeply. It had wanted to play with the neighbor's sock-footed cat, too, and now it was gone. They knew their child's looks by now.

The husband woke up screaming in the middle of the night, his inner thigh bit so hard it turned black. This, even though they'd taken to locking its bedroom door from the outside. They had forgotten the attic access in the closet. There came a moment— probably before the husband dragged the child, gnawing on his gloved hand, through attic insulation—when things shifted like a plank laying across a fulcrum, weight placed on one end. Happiness went away. Sleep was all they could think about. It would be nice to have friends over, but when you locked the thing in the dryer and pushed something heavy against the door, it banged and banged and rocked the whole machine and thumped and howled.

"He never called it a baby," they said. "He was careful not to."

The baby itself wasn't doing well. It had ceased smelling like cookies. Now, it smelled like whatever oily droplets the baby catcher had given to them in the woods—the way they'd smelled at first, before they mellowed into mushrooms and dirty leaves. Their child was not growing. Its plumpness was waning, its folds disappearing. Its skin looked yellow, and sometimes ashen.

•

They sat on the couch, in silence, until the Benadryl mixed into the bottle took effect and it stopped hurling itself against the closet door. As soon as it was out, they put it in a dog kennel, added a padlock, and set it in the backseat of the car. They drove.

At first they followed the grid they'd made on a map, covering two areas where they were sure they'd met up with him. They drove each row, each column. They abandoned the grid and drove in a widening concentric pattern. They abandoned and drove haphazardly. When it woke, they spiked the bottle again and let it suck through the locked gate of its cage. They slept for a few hours in the foul-smelling car. They woke early, drove all day.

They asked around. At every small-town tavern and barbershop. At little country stores in the middle of nowhere. They described him. Mostly, they got strange stares. But then, in a far-off region—had they crossed state lines?—people began to nod at them. One of the tiny towns had a grandiose name from found-ers' high expectations, and it was in this village, named for some Greek or Egyptian god (Serapis, maybe? Osiris?), people knew of the Babycatcher.

"I don't know his name," the woman at the diner told them. Many people in many little shops told them the same. "But I know who you're talking about."

"Tell him we're looking," they said. "If you see him, tell him we're desperate. The baby's life is at stake." The couple left their emails, their home address, their cell phone numbers.

The first message arrived for them at a butcher's shop, on a small scrap of paper handed to them by the bloody-aproned man behind the counter: *No refunds*, it read.

They left their own note: *Please just take it.*

They checked at the butcher's the next day, but there was no response. They left another note: *We think it's dying*

They couldn't find Wi-Fi or cell service, so they stopped at an ATM to check their bank balance. It was dangerously low. A bank teller from inside handed them a scrap of paper: *No guarantee. No refund. No returns.*

They scrawled their own note on a deposit slip: *We will pay you to take it.*

The local jeweler stopped them on the street as they passed his shop door. He handed them a map, drawn in what they now recognized as the Babycatcher's spidery script.

They followed it to the familiar gravel road, where they parked and continued on foot, carrying the kennel down game trails. When they got to the X, there was another set of directions drawn on a scrap of paper nailed to a tree. They followed these new direc-tions, down more game trails, down a tire-rutted dirt path.

They heard a motor and hid. A conservation officer in a jeep bumped slowly along the path. She wore a big Smokey the Bear hat, shotgun propped in the seat beside her. She stopped near where they crouched. She stood up and scanned the woods with binoculars. They knew what this meant. They did not move. It would be jail. The most horrible kind of jail. "But it's not really a baby!" they would argue. "It doesn't grow up!" Likely it wouldn't matter. It wouldn't live long enough to prove what it really was. They were sure she had seen them. They were sure she was deliberating how to apprehend them. But then the ranger drove on. Maybe she knew? Maybe once a month a couple walked through these woods with a kenneled thing (not a baby, as much as it looked like one) and there was nothing to do but let the couple leave it. Maybe she didn't blame them, considered them victims—maybe they were like addicts, the Babycatcher like the dealer. Maybe he was the poacher, they were the prey.

In any case, the conservation officer drove on.

The couple walked through the woods with the baby in the kennel. They followed the man's directions to where he'd drawn an X in the middle of a field, where there was a tree that had grown around and enveloped an old bicycle. *Leave it* was written in his strange chicken scratch on the note. In the middle of the field? They did. Next to the tree. With what little money they had in an envelope atop the cage. They waited. No one came. They couldn't just abandon the small thing in a kennel in the field. They still had no cell service. They watched from the woods. They checked on it once, squeezed food between the bars. After that it wailed for two hours. The couple dozed like babies in the leaves—that cry, that wail, had become their sleep trigger. Months and years later, the nights would seem so quiet they couldn't sleep.

When they woke up, dew drenched and mosquito-bitten, the kennel was gone.

RAY OF GOLDEN YOLK

ALONE ON THE FACTORY FLOOR, Ray presses his face to the viewer screen of the Egg-o-Scope, a piece of equipment that would look equally at home in an ophthalmologist's office or submarine control room. The rubber cushioning forms a seal around his eyes, like a diving mask. At the other end of the Egg-o-Scope, the part Ray thinks of as the business end, the whirring circuitry tapers to a fine point that looks like it could emit a laser beam. Here, just a few precisely calibrated centimeters from the Egg-o-Scope tip, eggs whiz by in single file on a high-speed conveyor. Ray looks for anomalies: double yolks, off-colored yolks, eggs-within-eggs, blood spots, meat spots, and so forth. In over ten years at his post, Ray has never encountered an anomaly. What Ray typically sees for eight hours per day, five days per week, is the illusion of a solitary egg, cross-sectioned and flawless—an illusion created in much the same way a twenty-four-frame-per-second film projection creates the illusion of a movie. The stationary egg's yellow dot of yolk, delicate white spirals of chalaza, crystalline layers of albumen, and pillowy air pocket are always perfectly balanced and gleaming, with nary a flicker to suggest it is not a single egg that has kept him company all this time but an image composed of hundreds of thousands of identical eggs per day, hundreds of millions of identical eggs per year.

But today is not typical. With still an hour and a half to go before lunch break, Ray flinches. The flinch sensors beneath the rubber cushioning react by flashing a red question mark on the screen. Ray stomps the floor pedal. The line halts. He pulls his face from the viewer window with a sucking sound and takes a deep breath. He flips the plastic lid that protects the glowing red button, and he pushes it. The conveyor reverses itself with a high-pitched whine then jerks to a halt, precisely aligning the flinched-at egg with the Egg-o-Scope tip so that the egg's insides will be visible on the screen. The red button has a delay time of one minute so the operator can investigate the egg and, in all likelihood, press the button a second time to cancel the alarm. Ray needs to hurry up and investigate now, but he is reluctant. He is not sure what he has seen, but the brief, subliminal glimpse has left him cold and full of dread. What he knows is that he does not want to see what he has almost seen ever again.

He could ignore his flinch and let the egg whiz along to its 99% post-consumer recycled fiber carton, but what if it's truly anomalous, as bad as he thinks, and someone cracks it open? He could also sit and wait and do nothing. But if the crowd from Upstairs comes all the way down to find a perfectly acceptable egg, then…well, bad news. Ray could end up out in the Chicken Shit. He is forty-four and aware that his reflexes began to sag some time ago. Operating the Egg-o-Scope is by far the highest-paying position at Golden Yolk for someone without a college degree, and Ray's daughter Soph is fifteen, which means four years of college tuition are right around the corner. His wife, Iris, loves her job as a birthing coach—a doula—although it doesn't even cover payments for their pre-owned Toyota. He can't afford to get caught with a faulty flinch response. Dread or no dread, he needs to verify this anomalous egg.

Ray peers in. The egg's interior is inky and it blooms, billows, churns, and swirls. He presses a thumb trigger and zooms close. There are shapes and contours like darkened brain folds, like a twisting cloud of eels. Maybe this is what a bad egg looks like? The whole mess beats twice—two strong contractions—and then quivers in aftershock, like a putrid Jell-O mold. It settles. It stills.

Then a yellow eye flicks open. It fills the window. A sliver of pupil, maliciously vertical, stares at him. The yellow is painful, like looking at the sun. There's a jolt against his forehead, like something sharp piercing the shell of his skull and shocking him in the middle of his brain. His vision goes dark, just a pale rainbow of twirling halos against a black screen. He stumbles backward, falls, and tweaks his tailbone on the cement floor. He rubs his closed eyelids, blinks as his vision slowly returns. But the afterimage continues to hover and glare.

The laboratory guys descend the metal staircase in their tie-dyed lab coats. The kaleidoscope of colors is supposed to make their department look friendlier, more approachable. Someone new is at the head of the pack. She's wearing a black suit, no lab coat, which is striking amidst the colorful swirl of her entourage. Apparently, the lab guys have all seen Ray fall on his ass. A few clap, a few chuckle, a few smile sheepishly and ask if he is all right. Ray rubs his tailbone. It doesn't hurt very badly, but it's less embarrassing to pretend it does.

"Quiet," says the woman at the head of the pack, and the lab guys snap to. "Get that checked out," she says to Ray. Her badge reads VISITOR, but she appears to be in charge, maybe even a division director from the parent company. What's confusing to Ray is that all the surrounding tie-dye says one thing while her flat voice and serious demeanor say another thing entirely.

"I'll be all right," says Ray.

"I know," says Visitor. "But that's not a request. It's policy. Send HR proof that you got it checked out. So, a bad egg?"

"That's an understatement," says Ray.

The guys in the rear of the group peak their eyebrows and grin at each other while Visitor wipes the rubber cushion with a disinfectant wipe and pokes her face into the viewer. While she looks, Visitor also opens a panel Ray has never seen opened before and fiddles with knobs and dials. "There you are," she says beneath her breath. The tie-dyed group fidgets expectantly. When Visitor is done, she steps aside to let the lab guys have a look. She opens a yellow Moleskine journal and writes notes in a swirl of dark ink.

"Well, what is it?" says Ray.

Visitor holds up one authoritative finger, then resumes jotting. Finally, the last guy in line readjusts the knobs and shuts the panel. He puts on a latex glove, removes the egg from the conveyor, and carefully drops it into a plastic baggie.

"We'll run some tests," the guy calls to Ray over his shoulder, already hustling away.

"Yes, we will," Visitor interrupts. "But actually, there's no evidence…what's your name?"

"Ray."

"Right. There's no evidence, Ray, to suggest that this is anything but perfectly all-natural. But you flinched, which is reason enough to investigate. The brain can see what the eye can't. That's why we pay you guys."

It's not clear to Ray who "you guys" are, since Ray works alone on the factory floor. Everyone else is Upstairs, or in an office. Ray worked on this very same floor back when it was bustling, but the original processing plant has been shut down for over a decade. Twenty-five years ago, Golden Yolk bought the infrastructure and, among other positions, hired two Egg-o-Scope operators, no experience necessary, just an intuitive response test. The other guy, Marc, ended up with a faulty flinch and got shipped out to the Shit, so now there is just Ray. The Egg-o-Scope is only operating at quarter capacity as it is, so unless business quadruples, Golden Yolk doesn't need anyone else.

"But tell me what you saw," says Ray. He tries so hard not to sound impatient that his voice comes out squeakily earnest.

"Just an egg," says Visitor "Although I calibrated the machine to view it using a more complex interface."

"Can I see?" says Ray. "Or maybe if you just looked at it the regular way…"

"No," says Visitor. "We have tests to run."

"Am I fired?" Ray asks. "Because I've never made a mistake before."

"No," she says. She smiles. The whole group smiles in response to her smile. "Even if this is nothing, it was a good save, Ray, okay? Or it might've been. Or it could be next time. Okay? You're important to the team. You didn't get this job by accident. You've got the reflexes, the intuition—well, it might not be *you*, exactly, but at least your ventromedial prefrontal cortex, nucleus accumbens, amygdala, and lateral temporal cortex know what they're doing. What I mean to say is: good save, Ray."

Visitor lifts her palm above her head, and after a moment Ray realizes what this means and slaps Visitor's raised palm with his own.

"That's the way," she says.

Before the group heads back upstairs, a few lab guys also offer Ray high fives, a few slap him on the back. One gives him a brief shoulder rub and ruffles his hair. "That's the way, Ray," they say. "Good save."

Though he knows Visitor and the lab guys have essentially pointed out a major fuckup and possible hallucination on his part, all the compliments and affectionate touching have Ray feeling a little better about it all. He plants his face into the viewer, stomps the pedal, and the eggs whiz along at high speed again. The afterimage of the halos and yellow eye hover faintly, but Ray looks through it. The illusion of a perfect, solitary, flickerless egg is before his eyes once more.

Until a few minutes later, when the egg blinks away for a split second and Ray flinches again. The red question mark flashes, and this time it happens instantaneously without even inspecting the egg—a lightning flash of yellow in the middle of his skull, a bunch of rotating dots, a splitting headache, and a surge of grief-like feelings that makes him moan out loud. He stomps the pedal and halts the line, cradles his head. Fuck, he thinks. His brow beads with sweat. He's sobbing and doesn't know why.

This can't happen. There is a future out in the Shit to avoid. There are Soph's tuition and Iris's job to consider. There is his fuckup of several minutes ago, his instant reaction of just seconds ago. Ray flips the lid and presses the glowing red button. The conveyor whines and reverses. He has one minute. He looks at the egg.

There it is again. The writhing. The darkness. The contraction. Ray knows what is next, and before the eye can flick open he hits the red button. He stomps the pedal and the conveyor whizzes back into high speed, and before him now is the same old, wonderfully correct egg that feels like coming home after a terrible, terrible vacation. He is not sure what, if anything, he has seen. He is not sure what, if anything, he has done.

He seems to have made the one-minute limit. The laboratory guys and Visitor do not descend the metal staircase. However, there is now the chance that in the next week or so a Golden Yolk customer, who will have paid an extreme price for a dozen of the most natural eggs on the planet, will crack a bad egg into a skillet and find something horrible sizzling there, staring back. Ray has either fucked up immensely or, only slightly better, gone insane. Either way, he fears his future is Chicken Shit. He sighs with worry, which triggers the red question mark. He turns it off. The perfect egg sits there, perfectly still. He feels sick to his stomach. He peels his face from the viewer and sits for a moment, taking deep breaths.

He reaches to scratch his ankle, and that's when he sees it. Down by his foot, on the cement floor, right under the panel Visitor opened, a golden bunny medallion glints on a ring of keys. Ray picks up the keys and medallion. They belong to Bob, Ray's supervisor, and to discover them lying about misplaced is a routine event. At the beginning of every week Bob leaves these keys somewhere and spends the rest of the week looking for them. Bob's wife is used to driving Bob to work. Ray has found Bob's keys in the parking lot, in the employee fridge and freezer, on the men's room sink and stall-door hook, and on every flat surface of the Egg-o-Scope and its environs. Finding them now feels almost like a return to normalcy. It's comforting.

The medallion isn't literally a bunny, but Ray doesn't know what else to call the shape. The first time he saw the keys, they were swinging on Bob's finger while Bob kicked back in his office chair, feet up on his desk, as is Bob's habit. Behind Bob, stacked in the office corner, was a tattered stack of nudie mags so old they predated Bob. The magazine on top had the old Playboy Bunny logo on it from long, long ago—so it was an instant, random connection. But the second time Ray saw the keys, sparkling on the parking lot asphalt where Bob had dropped them, the medallion looked like something else entirely, like half of a yin-yang, or an inverted comma with an extra eye-like circle. It's one of those shapes that asks the mind to mold it into whatever it wants.

Now, no more than ten minutes since the second anomalous egg, Ray flinches at a third and jerks back from the machine, headache and grief surging, afterimage burning. He grabs the egg. He cancels the alarm. He holds the egg above his head to smash it on the cement floor. He considers the Shit. Iris's job. Soph's tuition. He hesitates.

Ray is frozen like this when Bob comes out of his dirty office to make his supervisory rounds. On his index finger, Bob swings and jangles his set of master keys, hooked to the golden bunny medallion. Bob sees Ray. Bob's eyes get big: "Whoa! Whoa!" Bob yells, and he begins to run remarkably fast across the floor on stick legs that look like they shouldn't support his girth.

Ray pats his shirt pocket with his free hand to check that the keys he found, the ones that now appear to be swinging on Bob's finger, are still there. The egg, still held aloft in his other hand, slips from his grasp.

"Whoa!" Bob yells. He extends both hands, as if he could somehow dive and catch the egg from over ten yards away.

Ray bends deep at the knees, fumbles the egg hot-potato-style and then cradles it in his cupped hands, unbroken. For a moment he's stuck like this, in a deep squat, as if about to perform a complicated traditional folk dance. His back and knees sing out in pain. He collapses onto his ass, heart thumping.

"Damn good reflexes," says Bob. "What in the hell were you doing?"

Ray tries to explain, but he can't find the words. The best he can do is to extend the egg to Bob, who accepts it.

"Ray, Ray," Bob says with a hand on Ray's back. Ray knows Bob as a nice man, a guy who remembers when a worker has a sick kid and asks about the kid by name every day until the kid gets better. "Let's go sit in my office a minute," he says. He extends a hand and helps Ray up.

Ray dusts himself off. Bob swings the medallion and ring of keys wildly on his finger, his habit when worried or thinking. They slip off, fly, and scuttle across the cement into a shadowy heap of neglected old machine parts.

"Shit," says Bob.

Ray takes the identical keys out of his pocket. Bob makes a blank face and blinks his big eyes rapidly, as if Ray has just performed a magic trick. Then he takes the keys, examines them.

"Must belong to Upstairs," he says. "He taps the golden comma medallion. "Fancy key-ma-bob." He puts them back in Ray's pocket and pats them. "So I don't lose them," he says with a nod to the dark, dusty area of rusted parts. "Remind me and we'll interoffice them. Let's take a breather. Let's go talk. I have some theories. Let's figure out what this is all about."

"But your keys?"

"No, no. Let's not get distracted. I've got hunches for you to hear. The keys are okay over there. That's a good spot. I know pretty much where they are. Just don't let me forget."

•

Bob's office is a mess of metal furniture, dust, stacks of dirty magazines from predecessors past. They drink bourbon or something like it out of coffee mugs.

"It could be an experiment," says Bob after Ray has told him his story. Bob clears his desk by swiping his papers to the floor, and then he sets the egg down gingerly. It wobbles with the same perfect balance as a normal egg. "It could be they're upping the all-naturalness again." They watch the egg, and when it stops Bob pokes the egg with his finger and sets it back to wobbling. "I've been hearing things," he says. "On the group calls with other managers. Little mentions slipped in between other mentions."

Bob lets this simmer. Ray has to widen his eyes in frustration to prod Bob along.

"Okay, alright. I shouldn't be talking. All rumors. But I suspect these are non-eating eggs."

"Non-eating?"

"Non-eating. In the old days they'd grow medicines, vaccines and such, in these little guys. Lots of uses."

"You think what I described sounds like a medicine?"

"Well…" Bob makes a *stop busting my balls* face, followed by a *let me level with you* face. "What I think is you saw something maybe some people wanted you to see, and maybe a lot of other people didn't."

"Bob, you're gonna have to—"

"Spill the eggs. Got it. Listen, we both know GY is about as big as an endless string of corporate entities can get, and so it'll shock you zero percent that it's not always harmonious. From what

I hear? Way the opposite. Internal factions. Nigh on Civil War. You know the history—the original founding family ages ago. Shares passed down and split between second cousins, ninetieth cousins, and so far down the bloodlines that it's not even family at this point. Bunch of strangers. Some of them are bound to be oddballs by sheer probability. There's that legend of a whole division bequeathed to a, well, it's a goldfish in one version, a cat in another, amidst assorted other species. All this you've heard before."

Ray has heard none of this before—who would he have heard it from? But he doesn't like it one bit that part of the steady institution upon which his family depends is perhaps run by a who-knows-what-kind-of-animal—and why does he hope it's a cat and not a goldfish?

"The main thing being," continues Bob, "is that divisions run deep. Power struggles. All sorts of left hands hiding from right hands, etc. Amidst all this, you see what you see in the eggs, and at the same time we have a—I'm guessing you saw her?"

"Visitor?"

"Visitor." He lets the word sit. "What do you make of her?"

"Scary."

Bob guffaws. "Yeah. Oh, yeah. That's how you get to be a Big Boss. You be terrifying. I'm guessing she's full-on division head by the no-fucks-given way she carries herself. And you know what that means."

"I have no idea what any of this means."

"Well, me neither, not really, but it means the war has come to our doorstep, my friend. Something has gone horribly wrong, probably. Some big fuckup, maybe, and she's here to hide it. Or there's an equal chance something has gone horribly right and she's here to exploit it. Either way: hide or exploit; exploit or hide. She's a queen on this board and you—"

"Pawn."

"Not even. You wish. You're a lice—"

"Louse."

"Yes. Just a louse on the ass hair of a diseased, half-starved peasant about to be killed by an also diseased, half-starved foot soldier's servant of a pawn—and no offense! Me too. I'm just a bigger, older lice—louse."

Ray's heart is racing, forehead beading. "I'll be out in the Chicken Shit, then. That's what you're saying?"

"I don't know. Let's not go there yet. All I'm saying is: you stay out of it, Ray. Be invisible. That's all the protection we peasant's louses have. What I do know is this: had you smashed this egg on the floor?" Bob pokes the egg again for emphasis. "Upstairs would make me send you to the Shit. Or even worse, fire you outright. You might have to leave Golden Yolktown for Scrubland. Nothing I could do. So, you watch the eggs, and when you flinch you press the red button, Ray. Press the button. That's it. That's your job."

Ray hangs his head and nods. He feels exhausted. Bob creaks back in his desk chair. They sip their whiskey. Ray wonders if he should tell Bob that he let one go, a bad egg. They'd never find it now. They'd have to sift through a few thousand. Or throw them all away. They'd send him to the Shit for that, which was now sounding good compared to exile from the company town, out to Scrubland. Ray wants to say something to make it better, but nothing comes to mind.

Bob raises both hands. "But, hey. Maybe I'm overreacting. This *Visitor* has me all kebobbled. It could be simpler than all this. What if it's stress?" Bob raises his eyebrows and nods his head, making a *how about that?* face. "This could be a good egg here." He pokes. It wobbles. "Stress could be making *you* a bad egg *here*." Bob nudges his temple with a finger. "How are things at home?"

Ray senses he is being offered a plausible excuse, a way out, and is inclined to take it by describing every home-related stress he can think of, but Bob interrupts him.

"I don't need to know the details, Ray. It's none of my business. But stress or no stress—internal corporate Civil War or not—you're definitely rattled by the events that have transpired here today, and so my official position is for you to take the rest of the day off and take a PTO day tomorrow—Friday—to rest up. Enjoy a long weekend with your family."

"Thank you," says Ray. "But I think I'm okay now. I really can't afford it."

"Don't clock out," whispers Bob. "We'll do the PTO tomorrow off the record. This is me doing one of my boys a favor. I haven't stuck my nose in an Egg-o-Scope for a good while. If some new, wild mistake or crazy success is coming down the line, I wouldn't mind getting a look at it myself. It will help me procrastinate my paperwork." Bob glances at the floor, as if to verify his paperwork is still there. "Plus, I don't want to order up an official eval by Dr. Z. Gupta. That never goes well. I don't see the need for that if you get yourself some rest."

"What about my employee record?" asks Ray.

"Does it look like I know where to find your employee record?"

"Thanks, Bob. I could use the time. Think things through."

"Collect yourself, yes. Calm yourself, yes. But think about it? No no no. It will make things worse. Maybe you should see Dr. Z. Gupta on your own, off the record? This sort of thing is his area."

"What are you going to do with the egg?"

"Go home, Ray. Go on home."

•

Ray collects his lunch cooler from his locker. Outside, a dusting of snow covers the lot, but the sun is out and the snow is beginning to melt and glitter. He drives the family RV with the windows down and forces himself to sing along loudly to the country station. He can hear the RV's rattles and creaks over the music. It's an old beast of a machine, inherited from Iris's father, who'd poured love and mechanical ability into it, like he did with so many things. Along

with the RV, he'd left them a barn that held a restored antique tractor and other refurbished, useless oddities. The RV, though, turned
out to be a bit of luck. When Iris needed the family Toyota for her
doula practice, Ray swept the behemoth free of leaves and debris
from its spot in the big barn, alongside the tractor. He vacuumed
the remains of a mouse nest out of the engine, changed the battery
and a few sensor faults, and was surprised when the motor kicked
in with some sparks and belt squeaks and settled into an acceptable hum.

Ray sings all the wrong words to the country song but keeps
singing anyway. The roads from Golden Yolk to Golden Yolktown
slice through vast fields of grass, a byproduct of the egg business:
something has to be done with all the chicken shit. A special cohort
of lab guys developed a method for turning what could be an un-
sightly, stinky, community-relations problem into microorganism-
rich, organic sod fields that, even in mid-March, are already bright
green beneath the sparkling white powder. The fields smell sharply
of fresh-cut grass, even though they've never been mowed. Through
the large RV windshield, Ray sees a dim yellow spot hovering over
the road, encircled by faint, twirling halos of color. Soon the sod
will be sectioned off and rolled up like carpet to serve as organic
lawns or eco-roofs in distant corporate cities, beyond the Scrubland.

Far out in the green fields loom the domes of the chicken habi-
tats. They look like giant, half-buried Ping-Pong balls. It's hard
to tell their true size from the road, but Ray has heard that each
could hold several Golden Yolktowns. Within the domes, reads
the company literature, a chicken—or anything that breathes, really—is capable of living a life more natural than any place outside.
Humans have never been allowed inside except maybe, on rare
occasions, scientific specialists in custom bio-suits. The domes ex-
pensively recreate a small capsule of existence comparable to what
things were like before pollution, before us. Over in marketing,
words like "primordial" get bandied about.

The family farmhouse and barn, visible from a long way off, sits alone in a copse of trees surrounded by miles of Golden Yolk grass. Ray steers the RV into the driveway. Gravel snaps and pops under the tires. Iris grew up in this house. Ray courted Iris here in high school, and his own childhood home is two miles away and nearly identical, except that it's now leaning severely, inhabited only by owls, mice, and raccoons. Ray remembers the keychain medallion, pulls it from his pocket, and sets it in the cup holder so he'll remember to interoffice it tomorrow. Stay invisible. That's the plan. Invisible.

It has snowed more here. Through several sets of partially melted footprints marching across the front yard Ray can see early sparks of green. Most of the grass is still shriveled, gray, and dormant, but peppered throughout are thick, healthy, bright-green tufts that are unmistakably the same grass that grows out in the sod fields. Ray wonders if he should be glad that he's slowly getting a free, high-end lawn or worried that it's encroaching on its own.

Ray ducks just in time to avoid hitting his head on a sagging branch of the apple tree in the front yard. Hanging from the otherwise bare branch is a large red apple with a spot of melting snow nestled around the stem. Ray looks closely at the stem; because the apple is out of season, he half-expects it to be tied, glued, or otherwise artificially attached to the tree. It isn't. It looks real. Thick droplets of snowmelt trickle down the sides and drip from the bottom.

Ray has eaten apples from this tree his entire life. Iris's mother sent baskets of these apples to Ray's mother for baking apple pies. Ray has roasted these apples with cinnamon on sharpened sticks over fall bonfires. The tree has never grown an apple like this—so dark, so bloodred, so wildly out of season. He pokes the apple with his finger. It pendulums. The stem snaps. The bough lifts. The fat apple drops to the lawn.

Inside, Ray sets the apple on the round kitchen table and takes a seat, staring alternately at the apple and at Soph's tablet on the counter, playing what is either anime or manga, Ray can't remember which is which. The characters zing through the air with giant eyes, wielding swords. Soph enters the kitchen, sliding gracefully on the smooth floor in her socks. She takes a tub of mint chocolate chip from the freezer and eats it at the table, spooning directly from tub to mouth.

"You shouldn't have picked the apple," she says between licks of the spoon.

"How long has it been there?"

"I was going to take a video of it, but I didn't know how to make the apple look real. Who's to say I didn't just superglue it to the branch, you know? I didn't see it until this morning."

"Is it real?" Ray asks.

Soph bites a chunk from the apple and chews noisily. From the tablet comes a chiming sound, like glimmering coins, followed by characters squeezing their humongous eyes closed and laughing strangely. Soph closes the lid. The tablet sleeps.

"Tastes real," she says with her mouth full.

Her glasses have slid down, and she uses her tablet to push them back up. Ray hates Soph's glasses. There's something about the black, square frames that make Ray think she's mocking him most of the time. For one, they don't even have prescription lenses. They seem like a step toward something. Soph recently asked permission to streak her hair an array of unnatural colors. Right now it is long and brown and shiny, but she complains that it looks like a shampoo ad. Ray doesn't get it. Do they not advertise such hair because it is healthy and silky and shimmering and all that people hope for? Lately she's into inventing and drawing semi-comical tattoos, like fantasy world maps that use freckles, moles, hair, and scars as landmarks. She jokes about piercings in outlandish places like the bottom of her feet. Sometimes Ray isn't sure Soph is actually joking. He wonders how much longer he'll recognize her.

"Maybe this is the best apple I've ever had," she says. She bites again.

"I don't know," says Ray. "It's out of season. Doesn't seem right."

"Nah, bruh," she says. "Things change. Weird stuff gets discovered in the ocean. New jellyfish. Weirder squids. They look like aliens, but there they are. And if they're yummy, we eat them."

"Well, that's no deep-sea apple. If it's radioactive or genetically altered, you're going to grow a third hand on your back while you sleep."

"If I learned to write and tie my shoes with a third hand on my back, would I still be left-handed? I hope so. Left is my choice of direction in general. I always try to make counter-clockwise decisions." She takes another bite. Chews. "I heard the Henderson kids, from school, their cat got the flu or depression or whatever, and it ate all the kittens in the litter. And that Billy guy, the one who's now a Golden Yolktown security deputy? When he was a kid, he tied his gerbil spread-eagle to the top of his great-grandfather's antique, priceless Death Star toy, and when he got back from lunch it had gnawed its own arms and legs off. Oh, and I saw a clip once about a little girl that got either half or all eaten by an alligator in a hotel swimming pool."

She bites another crisp chunk of apple and adjusts her black glasses.

"I don't even know what you're talking about," says Ray.

"I'm just saying, you know, nature," she says. "It's weirder than you'd think."

Ray feels like he has lost an argument without even knowing the general topic of the argument.

"Why haven't you asked me yet why I'm skipping school?" she asks him.

Ray looks at the clock. It's one p.m. He's home hours earlier than usual, but Soph is always home before him on Thursdays, so it didn't occur to him she shouldn't be.

"I have a big, big problem," she says.

"What is it?"

"I don't know if I can trust you."

"Of course you can."

"Wait a minute," she says. "If I give you time to imagine how bad it is, then maybe what I tell you won't be as bad as what you imagined. But it is really. I'll be right back." She goes to the bathroom.

"Soph!" he shouts after her. But he knows his shouting hasn't meant anything to her for years. Ray knocks on the bathroom door.

"I'm not coming out until you go back to the table and imagine," she says.

Ray sulks back to the kitchen. He tries not to imagine, but he can't help it. He already feels like crying. What keeps coming to mind is that his daughter has been raped, and he wants to kill the motherfucker responsible. He can't picture any of the boys in her class. Soph has never been on a date. The only person Ray can visualize is the principal with his blow-dried hair. Ray imagines taking a bat to the man's face, the hair flying all about. But no matter how hard Ray works on his visualization of whacking the principal in the face, the principal stays unharmed and smiling, and his hair keeps landing perfectly in place. Ray feels the painful yellow eye flick open inside his skull, twirled by sad, colorful halos.

"Soph! Come on, please!" he calls.

"There's no sex involved," she says. "I know that's what you were thinking. Do you feel better?"

"Actually, I do," he says.

Soph sets something on the table. Ray looks at it for several moments without making the connection. It's a pregnancy detector, the AI kind, and it clearly reads *pregnant.*

"I don't understand," says Ray. "Who does this belong to?"

"Somehow," she says, "me."

Ray reaches to pick it up, then puts his hand back down because he doesn't remember how they work exactly, or where it's been. He feels like the right thing to do is to slap her. He has to do something with his hands. He rubs his fingers through his thinning hair. He does this several times, looking at the detector.

"Who is the boy?"

"That's what I'm saying," she says. "I've never done, you know...*it*. But I haven't had my period for almost two months. I've been vomiting. I've got tender boobs. Headaches. Backaches. Cravings. I think something tricked my body into thinking it's pregnant. So I ordered the detector. But it can't be real. It's a freak allergic reaction, maybe."

"Soph, listen," he says. He tries to use a wise, fatherly voice, something he heard on the programming of his youth, but it's not sounding right. It occurs to him that this is one of those times— maybe *the* time: what he does right now will make him either a good father or bad father. "There's only one way these things happen," he says. "I'm not mad at you. Don't tell me a name if you don't want to. But let's be truthful."

"I *am* being truthful," she says.

"Soph." The impulse to slap her returns. He runs his hands through what's left of his hair again. "Look at me like a real person and take those ridiculous glasses off."

"No."

Ray grabs the glasses and pulls them off. Her face looks naked and unprotected now. He realizes for the first time that this is why she wears them, for protection. A kind of force field between herself and the world. They help her show her face to the meanest kids at school. He has never thought about it this way before. He feels like an asshole.

"Dad, you're an asshole!" she says. She is crying now.

"I'm sorry," he says. He holds the glasses delicately with two hands and slowly extends them. She turns her head at first, but then she lets him place them on her nose and over her ears. He pats down her hair where he messed it up. He wipes a tear out of his eye. "How am I supposed to believe you?"

"You just are," she says. "That's what you do."

"Okay," he says. He knows this is not the time to be a hardass. Whatever is done has already been done. This is when fathers lose their daughters, when there's nothing left to do but be kind and they just don't know how. If she needs a story, he'll play along for now. The story is maybe like the glasses. If he's patient, maybe he'll get behind the force field. "I believe you," he lies.

"Really?"

"Yes. You're my daughter."

"Okay, then," she says. "Good."

"Have you told your mother?"

"No. She's into, you know—she's a baby person. Births and infants are what she loves. And no way am I keeping this fake baby I didn't make. She'd either slap me, or be weirdly happy and make a birthing plan, or it would break her heart. You're more predictable. You just get all sad and worried and love me anyway."

Ray can't help but feel satisfied that Soph chose to tell him instead of Iris.

"Don't be so happy about it, Dad. You're both better and worse than each other in different ways. I hate it when you guys compete. I wish I wasn't an only child."

Ray is embarrassed now. He feels like not just an asshole, but a transparent, predictable asshole.

"So I'm the softy?" he asks.

"It's not the worst thing you can be."

"I don't know," he says. "So what do we do?"

"Take me to a doctor," she says. "I could go myself, I suppose. But I'm scared. I want you to drive me. You have to come with me."

"That sounds like the best idea," he says. He's relieved to pass the mess onto someone who has a degree and a professional obligation.

"I already made an appointment with Dr. Z. Gupta. It's tomorrow. I figure you could take me during your lunch."

"I'm taking tomorrow off, so I have time."

"Thanks, Dad."

"What are we going to do about your mom?"

"Nothing," she says. "Not until we have an answer."

"She's not going to be happy about that," he says.

"Maybe deep down she knows that she's not the best parent for this job."

Ray doesn't think so. He doesn't argue. Mostly he's just glad it's not he who has to break the news to Iris. Soph's fake glasses have gone a little cockeyed again, so he reaches out and straightens them.

When she leaves to do her homework, he doesn't know what to do with himself, so he bites at the apple mindlessly. When he's down to the core, he looks at it and sees, or feels, the faint flick of a yellow eye. His mind can't help but place it inside of his daughter, an unwanted growing thing, and also inside himself, as the apple he just ate. He runs upstairs to the master bathroom and throws up.

•

The sound of tires on the gravel driveway wakes Ray up a little after nine p.m. He is curled up on top of the comforter. He last had sex nearly six months ago, after a dinner out to celebrate the completion of Iris's advanced-level doula training and her promotion at the birthing center. She assists nurse-midwives and helps women birth their babies at the center or at home in giant tubs of water, without epidurals, the same way she gave birth to Soph. She's strong and good at her job, but she comes home wanting silence, a cup of herbal tea, and sleep. Ray remembers getting in the tub with her, supporting her weight with the crook of his elbows under her armpits while she breathed and moaned, and when she comes home from work now he can see the exhaustion and fatigue of labor all over her.

He hasn't brought up sex, the absence of it, because he wants to assume her job is at fault. He doesn't want it to be that she doesn't love him anymore. She probably still loves him. They talk about the bills they can barely pay and how to get on your hands and knees to flip a baby into position. He means to talk about other things, but the days accumulate and make it harder. She loves Soph, otherwise she wouldn't get exasperated about screen time and studying for the college entrance exams. She never gets exasperated at Ray about anything, which worries him.

He pretends to be asleep and listens to her run the faucet and fiddle with things in their bathroom. She takes so long that he falls asleep for a while and then wakes up again.

"Ray!" she whispers loudly. He fakes sleep. He's not sure why. Her voice sounds like she needs to talk to him badly. There's something about this that he likes, that he wants to extend. She approaches the bed. She pauses. "Please, wake up."

"I'm awake," he says.

"I'm pregnant," she says.

"It's not you," he says. He's still not entirely lucid. For a moment it makes a kind of sense that Iris has confused Soph's positive pregnancy test with her own. But he's waking up now, and he knows this can't be true.

She sits beside him on the bed and holds a bouquet of pregnancy detectors in front of him. "I bought six. Three different brands," she says. "I mean. I'm over forty. I didn't think—and we've been more than careful."

She looks at him, nervous. Her eyes and hair are brown and beautiful and kind. He touches her back because he doesn't know what to do. It feels good to touch her like this.

"Should I be scared or excited?" she says.

Ray feels trapped. Iris has referred to sex of which he has no memory. After what happened at work today, he is not in a state of mind to trust his own senses. Iris is not a liar. She once told him, after he asked, that it was true his thinning hair made him significantly less sexy. He has never known her to make things up. If she thinks they have been having sex, then to confess not having any memory of sex with her for the last six months is a realm of trouble he is unprepared for.

"We'll be okay," he says, even though he's not sure.

"That's a start." She pauses. "So how bad is this?"

He knows he should suspect his wife of having an affair. But if Iris were cheating and wanted to get away with it, then it would make more sense to have a secret abortion than attempt to convince someone you haven't had sex with that you have indeed had sex. No one would believe that could work. Except maybe it *is* working. Maybe she had an affair and got pregnant and loves babies so much she wants to keep it? Maybe her plan is preposterously brilliant?

"Iris, we've—I guess we've…well, maybe we've been going through a rough patch." He can't quite bring himself to say what he wants to say. Feels too explosive, too life-altering.

She bursts into tears. Ray doesn't think she hears anything he's saying. She's shaking. Maybe she isn't lying? It feels like she's being honest, in his gut. He doesn't think lying is something that would occur to her. If she wanted to have an affair, the Iris he knows would blurt it out and make him discuss it at length. But this leaves him in a weird place with no answer. He's not sleepy, exactly, but he wants badly to sleep now, just to turn his mind off. Like Soph, maybe Iris needs to hold onto a maybe-false story to get through for now—or in any case, Ray does. He needs a story badly, something that will let him sleep.

He smiles. He rubs her back, puts his arm around her, squeezes her gently. "Hey," he says. "It's not like we're kids. We'll be okay. We can do this." He doesn't know what *this* is—it might be a much harder and less happy *this* than he's suggesting with his voice. Iris smiles. They hold each other. Then Ray thinks of Soph having a baby at the same time Iris has a baby, which means there will be two babies whose relationship is aunt to niece. This is exhausting.

"Is there a way that this could be good for us?" she asks.

"Yes," he says. "Yes."

And then Iris kisses him on the mouth—with passion and her tongue and everything—and that night they make love for the first time in nearly six months, so far as he can remember.

•

Later that night Ray tosses and turns and writhes in his sleep. He wakes up at some unknown hour sprawled across the width of the bed, alone in the dark. Iris must have fled to the couch. In a subsequent dream, the yellow eye flicks open. It continues to open and open. It widens and intensifies until he realizes that it's his own eyes that are open. The sharp yellow disc of morning sun glares through the bedroom window. He is late for work.

He is glad to be in a rush. A step or two behind feels like the perfect place to be just now: free from the obligation to think. He picks up yesterday's clothes from the floor and puts them on. He plunks a few ice cubes into a cup of coffee and slurps it. Iris is already at work. Soph sits at the kitchen table.

"Get to school," he says.

"Not going, remember?" she says through a mouthful of yogurt. "It's Friday. You took today off." She points her spoon at him. "Mom's pregnant too, isn't she?"

"What are you talking about?" he says. *Shit*, he thinks.

Soph's smirk tells him that his inexpert feign is actually a confirmation.

"I can hear most of what you guys say through the air vents," she says. "I don't even have to try. Mom left her receipt in the plastic bag in the kitchen trash. She bought pregnancy detectors in bulk. Plus, she left you this note. You're supposed to meet her at Dr. Z. Gupta's at 9 a.m. That's going to be weird, huh? Both of us going to see him on the same day? What do you think now? It's the apple. The grass. The assholes you work for have fertilized us. Don't forget my appointment."

He looks at his watch. Iris's appointment is in ten minutes. "I'm late," he says.

"Ha," she says. "Not as late as some of us."

•

Dr. Z. Gupta's medical facility is on the edge of town, abutting the fields of grass. It's part of a larger medical complex—a kind of corporate hospital slash research center—that also houses the birthing center where Iris assists the nurse-midwives. Before Golden Yolk bought the town and named it, unimaginatively, Golden Yolktown, it was one of the last remaining independent municipalities in the region—albeit one that was slowly getting subsumed by Scrubland.

There are still some remnants of that former existence. Across the street from the hospital is an old-fashioned strip mall that houses a long-shuttered, ancient movie rental shop, an out-of-business Chinese place, and a store that Ray can't even imagine what it might've been—the letters fell off the building long ago, leaving just the outlines of *Comic + Vape*. It's all from well before Ray's time, residue from other eras, like the half-buried railroad tracks at the edge of town that lead off into the vast Scrubland.

Visible beyond the strip mall is the original courthouse dome, part of the central town square. Like the strip mall, the downtown shops are mostly empty. The hospital facility, though, is brand new, gleaming with shiny glass and metal, and wildly out of place.

At the reception desk Ray learns that Iris has already checked in. A nurse leads him down a corridor to an examination room. En route, he glimpses the Big Boss from the day before, walking briskly with a fashionable corporate bag on her arm, the VISITOR name badge pinned to her gray jacket. Ray considers ducking out of sight—he doesn't want to get in trouble for his off-the-books PTO—but decides to fake confidence and acknowledges her with a nod instead. She either doesn't see him or ignores him. Inside the exam room, Iris is in a gown, perched on a bed covered with a thin sheet of paper. It crinkles loudly every time she moves.

"Have you seen the doctor yet?" he asks.

"Briefly. He sent me around the circuit for a battery of tests."

"Is everything okay?"

"Who knows? They always act like everything is ordinary. It's not their womb. Even cancer is ordinary in these places. I should be seeing a naturopath. And I would, if there was one."

In Iris's pessimistic albeit probably accurate statement about the normalcy of cancer, Ray finds hope. He hopes his family's peculiar tragedy will, from the standpoint of medical science, fall within the range of pretty ordinary. He hopes not to be alone in this, to learn of similar documented cases. Here are people who can reduce such events to tests, who can reason through them and offer explanations. However, to get the explanation he is seeking he will have to express his doubts about the nature of the pregnancy. He doesn't know how he will express these doubts without devastating Iris.

Dr. Z. Gupta enters, a clipboard tucked under one arm. He shakes both of their hands before slathering his own with a sharp-smelling gel, which he continues to rub in while perched on a shiny silver stool.

"A new life is blossoming inside you!" he says.

Iris reaches out to Ray, and they clasp hands. Ray is smiling because Dr. Z Gupta and Iris are smiling, but also because Dr. Z. Gupta looks exactly like the man Ray needs: He wears a gleaming lab coat all the brighter against silky brown skin; his jet hair is streaked white at the temples; polished instruments glimmer all around him; his overseas English is as crisp as distilled water; the halos that hover in front of his eyes seem less like wireless spectacles than open windows to the truth. Here is a man who can see clearly. An angel of the rational.

"I want you to see something," says Dr. Z. Gupta. "A new technology that makes us *quite* proud."

The apparatus pulls down from the ceiling like a periscope. It is not unlike the device the optometrist uses when his eyes are on one side, yours on the other, except in this case Iris's womb is tucked snugly against one side of the device while Dr. Z. Gupta peers and adjusts switches and dials. It takes a long time, and Ray imagines Dr. Z. Gupta zooming in toward the distant disc of a new galaxy, until he sees a solar system situated on the tip of one of the galaxy's spiral arms, and then a moon circling a planet in that solar system, and finally a shiny pebble in a crater on that moon.

"Ah, beautiful!" Dr. Z. Gupta keeps saying.

"Is this a new ultrasound?" Iris asks.

"No, no, no. Very different," says Dr. Z. Gupta.

"It looks a little like my Egg-o-Scope at work," says Ray, and then he feels like an idiot because obviously they would be nothing alike.

"Different versions of nearly the same technology," says Dr. Z. Gupta. "We have the same parent company. In fact, here we are looking at an egg as well, in the very early stages, blossoming into life. Let me show you."

The lights go out and a long, thin screen on the wall flicks on. It is immediately clear why the doctor has chosen a floral comparison; at first glance the image seems to be an out-of-focus field of wildflowers. Fuzzy circles in a wide array of colors open into expanding rings. The colors of each ring change, new circles appear, and the field seems to slowly rotate and spin on a gentle, kaleidoscopic current.

"You could almost hang this in a museum," says Dr. Z. Gupta.

"But it's only the everyday beauty of the human body."

Ray finds himself mesmerized. Here it is. Whatever it is. Mysterious. But visible. He feels in his chest a kind of warmth, almost a vibration, what might be heartache or longing; this usually only comes to him with sad music, in response to the sounds, not the words, although sometimes the sounds of the words. He has felt it when he misses someone, especially Soph or Iris.

But also: he has seen something like this before. In the halos that swirled in his vision after the yellow eye flicked open. That was a somewhat different pattern that yielded a different feeling— a profound grief instead of this pleasant yearning. Maybe that is the difference between bad egg and good egg? Ray needs Iris's to be a good egg.

After they have all looked on at length, in wonderstruck silence, Dr. Z. Gupta turns the lights back on. Ray looks at Dr. Z. Gupta in a way that makes the doctor raise one eyebrow slightly. Ray wants to be convinced. He doesn't know what he has seen. It in no way proves his paternity. But whatever it was, it was beautiful. Ray wants to claim it. He feels like it must be his. He has heard that mothers recognize their own children, even if those children are forty and have been missing for thirty-nine years. A sixth sense. Basic animal instinct. Call it what you will. When he watches the colors swirl—what would be just an abstract mush in another context—something inside him responds. Viscerally. He feels something. But in truth, if it comes down to truth, he has no idea at all.

"What can you tell from this, Doctor?" asks Iris.

"Officially I have to send it in to be read by the technician, but I'll tell you off the record. What we're looking at is way down deep in mitochondrial and eukaryotic process and subprocesses, as nucleotides form genes, as life gets the special spark that is life. A more detailed look than we've ever been able to see before. Of course, it's not one to one. The AI is rendering it into something we can visualize, and the final imagery needs AI assistance to fully interpret. But here it is, visible for the first time. At this early stage, with this device, one looks for symmetry, for smooth, rhythmic patterns. Regular shapes. Whereas things that look irregular to the eye, odd shapes or arrhythmic movements, are clear signs of trouble. My inclination is that all seems healthy here, but we'll have to wait for the AI analysis. I wouldn't have shown it to you if I suspected a problem. Problems are ugly."

Ray walks Iris back to the adjacent birthing center, and Iris talks about things like names, cloth diapering, and hypnobirthing methods. She seems happy. Ray wants to ask her how and when they conceived this baby, and to tell her he has no memory of it, but this is definitely the wrong time. Ray wonders if it will always be the wrong time from here on out. He wonders if doubt will be a permanent condition, if it will ruin his life.

•

Less than two hours later, Dr. Z. Gupta delivers nearly the same lines to Soph: "You could almost hang this in a museum. But it's only the everyday beauty of the human body."

A model of professionalism, Dr. Z. Gupta seems unfazed by Ray's awkward position. Ray doesn't know what to make of this. Does Dr. Z. Gupta's crisp, unconcerned manner mean that this is normal? Ray has changed his mind and no longer wants Dr. Z. Gupta to find this normal. He wants the doctor to drop his jaw at the fact that Ray's family is doubly knocked up. A doubly knocked-up family, especially mother and adolescent daughter, is supposed to make the jaw drop. There are supposed to be frantic nurses who gossip and snicker a bit too loudly. There should be a suspicious company social worker or HR officer nosing around, insinuating things. Where are the GY detectives who should be roughing him up with questions, questions he wishes a roughing-up could help him answer? But there is only cool Dr. Z. Gupta, who acts like it is none of his business. A certain percentage get cancer. Certain families get doubly knocked up.

Soph interrogates Dr. Z. Gupta about the possibility of spontaneous pregnancy, and Dr. Z. Gupta nips the discussion in the bud. He explains that, yes, there are limits to scientific knowledge, but nevertheless the impossibility of what she's suggesting should for the purposes of their discussion be considered a well-established fact. Yes, he agrees, female mice have been shown to be capable of reproducing without males, but only in controlled laboratory settings that don't extend to teenage girls in rural Corpo-Agzones surrounded by leagues of Scrubland. Yes, he agrees, Soph might very well be intact, in the hymeneal sense of the word, but this doesn't rule out any of the types of sexual activity that can lead to conception, and certainly isn't evidence of spontaneous pregnancy. With extreme patience, Dr. Z. Gupta answers all of Soph's fairly belligerent questions.

"Then if I understand you correctly, Doctor," says Soph, "all evidence *still* points to this as a legitimate case of spontaneous pregnancy. Since you really don't know everything there is to know."

Dr. Z. Gupta looks amused. "I'm afraid we'll just have to disagree," he says with no trace of anger or defensiveness. The man does not seem capable of losing his cool.

"Well, I didn't make it, so I don't want it," says Soph, pointing at the screen. "I mean, what am I supposed to feel after looking at this? It's like the 'reels' old people of yore used to watch on their 'social media.' You show me colorful AI-enhanced swirls and I'm supposed to believe *that's* a beautiful work of art inside me or whatever. How do you know what colors are inside me? Why don't you just add a soundtrack and claim that there's some mood music in there? Or maybe you could dance the feelings of the dividing cell cluster? This is all a giant guilt trip. You could play this exact clip to everyone who comes in here and nobody would know the difference. It makes me not trust you."

Ray is pretty sure that what he sees on the screen this time looks different than what he saw last time. The colors are the same, but perhaps heavier on reds and blues. And a looser swirl pattern, maybe? But he can't say for certain.

"I assure you there's a clinical reason for everything you see," says Dr. Z. Gupta. "It's for determining health, and it was developed for analysis rather than aesthetics. But if it happens that you, like many people, find that the deep subprocesses of cells growing healthily into an infant are pleasing to the eye, then you'll have to explain that phenomenon for yourself. I can't."

"I guess that's my point too," says Soph. "Turn it off. I want to go over my options."

They kick Ray out for this discussion, but it looks to Ray like she has already made her decision. Ray is thankful not to have to hear the decision out loud. Maybe at this very moment Soph is dropping the spontaneous pregnancy story and telling Dr. Z. Gupta the truth. In which case, Ray feels glad to have been spared that too.

•

When the appointment is over, Ray and Soph walk to the RV together in silence. They sit in the cab and stare out at the fields through the big windshield. In the far distance, beyond the fencing, barbed wire, and watchtowers, he can just barely see the landscape shift from green to the dried-out, dead-looking expanse of Scrubland.

"I thought it was a mistake. A false pregnancy. I didn't believe it could really be true," says Soph. She picks up the medallion from the cup holder and dangles it in front of her.

"Director's key," says Ray. "I need to give it back."

She's looks at it, and Ray thinks she hasn't heard him.

"Tadpole," she finally says, her voice distant. "Maybe." She sets it back down in the cup holder.

"Well," says Ray. He places his finger on the start button, then looks at her before powering on the RV. He doesn't know what to say. "What can I do? What do you need?"

Soph is still looking out at the grass. "I'm okay," she says, almost a whisper. Ray pushes the button. Cool air blows quietly out of the vents. She turns her eyes from the grass to Ray's eyes and opens her mouth to say more, but something has switched in her. Her eyes squint together and leak tears. What comes out is sob after sob.

Ray reaches across the space between seats and holds her as tight and well as he can in the RV cab, tears soaking his shoulder. "Oh, daughter," he says, "my daughter." The wind blows patterns into the fields of grass. Funnels of dust plume and twirl over the distant Scrubland.

•

That night Ray lies awake in bed. He can't stop seeing the yellow eye's vertical pupil, the kaleidoscopic swirl of unexplained pregnancies. What if what Soph said is true, and Golden Yolk has fertilized them? Ray thinks of the anomalous egg taken Upstairs for tests. What else might be up there? He thinks of Visitor's golden tadpole, or bunny, in the RV cup holder. Trespassing—a break-in—would go beyond the Chicken Shit. It could be a banishable offense. No more safety of the Corpo-Agzone. They might open the gates, push him and his family out into Scrubland. Are the rumors true, that people had learned to survive out there by doing horrible, unimaginable things? Ray doesn't want to know. But it doesn't make sense that the fences and barbed wire are to keep people *in*, and the watchers in the towers are always looking *out*. Ray sits up and scoots to the edge of the worn-out bed. It squeaks when he stands up. Iris rolls into the comfy, sagging middle of the mattress. Her breathing is deep and peaceful.

Out in the hallway, Ray steps on the faint remnant of stars. Soph is the lightest sleeper imaginable, and when she was a colicky, unsleeping infant it seemed like anything would wake her—a distant dog's bark, a shift in bed, a sniffle, the wind. The floorboards in the hallway of the farmhouse seemed fine during the day, something you never thought about, but at night when you rose to pee or get a drink they were a symphony of creaks, a minefield of missteps that would wake the kraken. The glowing star stickers on the floor were Iris's idea. They spent one morning walking paths through the farmhouse in search of quiet spots, squeakless patches. When they found one—few and far between—they stuck a star there, the kind meant for a kid's bedroom ceiling. Silent, glowing footholds in the dark.

Now the stars are nearly gone. Years of footsteps, the vacuum cleaner, mop, and broom have slowly peeled them up. Ray can't even remember when they went from glowing stars to fainter stars to sticky residue invisible to the eyes but felt by bare toes in the night. Even now he imagines he still sees them there on the floor, although it's an illusion, a glimmer of moonlight bleeding through the curtains. They still glow in memory and habit. Down the stairs, Ray steps silently from long-gone star to long-gone star, his muscles remembering these steps without effort, this dance he's performed for so long. By the time he reaches the bottom, he feels the weight of it in his chest, the memories of this home where Iris grew up, where Soph was born, where they became a family.

Outside, Ray takes the bunny from the RV cup holder, tosses it on the passenger seat of the Toyota. He puts the car in neutral and rolls it down the gravel driveway before he starts it. He drives to Golden Yolk. Moonlight glistens on the grass tips and brightens the domes, aglow like so many half-buried moons. He parks the car behind a tottering stack of ancient pallets and uses his regular key to enter through the side door into the defunct employee locker room. Out of habit, he props the door open with a trashcan for keyless Bob, then catches himself and rolls the can aside.

On the factory floor, the silhouette of the Egg-o-Scope crouches over the conveyor line, as familiar as an old hat or coat you've worn your feelings into. "Hello?" Rays says to the immense darkness. All is quiet. Ray places one foot on the bottom metal step going Upstairs and waits. He listens. He thinks about the monthly payment on the second mortgage, how much damage just one missed paycheck would do. He grips the bunny in his pocket like a talisman, although it's more like the opposite—it pulls him into trouble, incriminates him. Up he goes.

The metal door at the top of the stairs has no window, no keyhole. It scrapes open with a tug. Beyond it is a short skywalk to the next building. The glass-and-metal bridge spans a narrow alley of weeds, gravel, and rusty electrical boxes. The door at the other end has a tadpole-shaped sensor, and when Ray touches Visitor's medallion to it, the glass doors slide apart. A fluorescent light turns on overhead, motion-triggered. He stands before a greeting station, the sort of desk where an administrative assistant would work. He wipes his sweaty hands on his pants. The doors slide closed behind him. It's air-conditioned up here, and clean, and even if the carpet and walls and accent paintings are a little generic, a little corporate, everything here is *nice*. It's a whole other world Upstairs.

Ray creeps along the carpeted hallways of office doors and, beyond, the tiled hallways of laboratories. He's not sure if he should tiptoe, crouch, and peek around corners or walk with bravado, as if he belongs here. He ends up strutting down the long stretches of open hallway like he imagines an executive would strut, only to drop into a squat and hunch into a ball at every imagined noise or movement. Alternating between strutting and squatting, Ray progresses hall by hall, triggering overhead lights that flicker on ahead of him. Behind him, the hallways gradually darken.

Ray looks for the egg, for anything anomalous. There are more laboratories than he expected. They're visible from the hallway, to either side, through giant windowpanes. Ray peers in. In one lab, an elaborate glassware edifice of beakers and tubes brings to mind an architectural model of a crystalline city: a sparkling palace, a vitreous roller coaster, glittering bridges, transparent spires. Another lab bursts with plants growing hydroponically beneath lights. Head-sized flowers bloom in myriad colors, arm-length leaves unfurl, and spiked seeds the size of basketballs dangle from limbs. Mostly, though, the labs don't look as Ray imagined they would. He pictured the ethereal atmosphere and dramatic lighting he knows from pharmaceutical advertisements and shows about crime scene forensics. He imagined a mad scientist's laboratory of half-human, half-chicken creatures afloat in cylinders, poked full of tubes. Instead, the Upstairs labs are more like scaled-up versions of the community college lab Ray studied in for half a semester before he dropped out to find work. Ray peers from window to window. The answers are here, right in front of him, but far above his pay grade, well beyond his years of schooling, out of reach.

He enters exactly one lab—the tadpole turns the sensor green, the door clicks open—and he chooses it for its wall of serious-looking refrigerators. Eggs go in the fridge, and here are fridges. When he opens the doors, though, there aren't anomalous eggs inside or normal eggs or any eggs at all. The shelves hold racks of color-coded vials filled with who-knows-what brown, viscous fluid. Nearby, on a counter, several squat gray machines are pocked with vial-sized holes. There is an adjacent printer and stack of printouts. Ray scans the pages, which contain lists of numbers. He could look at them the rest of his life and still not know what they mean.

An abrupt noise—a whoosh and a clunk—makes Ray duck and crouch. He waits. He peers over the counter. On the laboratory wall is the send-and-receive point of a pneumatic tube, not unlike the ones his grandmother told him were phased out during her own childhood, when they had literal, physical money stores called banks and drive-through tellers who used to suck coins and bills and things back and forth. This tube has just shot out a bullet-shaped metal cylinder. Ray twists it open. Its interior slots are filled with color-coded vials. While he's looking at these, a second cylinder blows through the tube and thunks down right in front of him. It brings to mind a rainbow-coated lab guy, maybe not so far away, who has pressed a button to send it here. It also brings to mind another colorful lab guy, at this end of the tube, expecting the delivery. Maybe this second guy will pick up the cylinder in the morning, or—and this version is vivid, real or imagined footsteps in the hall, getting closer—maybe this guy is coming right now.

Ray doesn't run back to the sky bridge. He does his quietest half-jog. He lopes while he creeps. He crouches at corners, noses his head around. He wants only to go home, tuck himself next to Iris in their sagging bed, and keep paying their second mortgage on time for as many months as he can. The tiled hallways of laboratories transition to the carpeted hallways of office doors. Ray stops to catch his breath, tame his panicking heart, and get his bearings. The bridge is close now, he thinks, down the longish hallway to the T, and then left to the greeting desk. He creep-lopes a few yards at a time, in fits and starts, stopping to listen to footsteps that are either imaginary or Ray's own or the lab guy's.

Scared and snailing along, Ray sees an office door nameplate that stands out among the many unfamiliar names and titles. VISITOR, it reads. Ray pauses. He hesitates. Home and safety are down the hallway, left at the T, and across the bridge. At the same time, a real or imaginary lab guy could be rounding the corner at any moment, which makes the hallway ahead feel infinitely long, and which also makes Ray feel utterly exposed, with nowhere to hide— except that here is a door to duck into, a door that might reveal what he came to see in the first place.

Ray places the tadpole. The door unlatches. He closes it softly behind him.

•

Inside, he breathes a deep breath. A familiar, kaleidoscopic glow bathes the room in a shifting rainbow of colors. It's soothing, like a nightlight. Clipped to the back wall, like X-rays, are a few dozen colorful swirling patterns that Ray recognizes from Dr. Z. Gupta's office. They spin slowly, prettily, and the intensity of their light darkens the rest of the room. Ray makes out a desk to one side, a meeting table, chairs, and couch to the other side. Ray approaches the prismatic wall and touches a sheet. He holds it between his thumb and forefinger. They're thin—not paper-thin, but film-like—and yet the images churn and ripple, like video. All of the screen-sheets have notations on them, written in fine-tipped marker. Some of the ripples and eddies have been circled and measured.

On the round meeting table, glowing less brightly, is a high-definition aerial map made of the same screen-paper, also annotated and labeled. The markers sit on the meeting table, and beside the markers is an abandoned mug of tea next to Visitor's yellow Moleskine journal. Ray knows the map's topography instantly, recognizes the roads cutting through the fields of grass. A few of the domes are circled in one of three colors, and a few are X'd out. Each is labeled with a *p* followed by a number, as in p100, p101, and so on. Ray looks again at the wall of rotating colors and, amidst the mess of other notations, sees these same numbers clearly in the top left corner of each: p100, p101….

There are three exceptions, outliers, on the end. One of these has Iris's birth date in the upper left corner, another Soph's, and the other his own. Ray takes these. It doesn't occur to him that he shouldn't. The swirling in his hands, even if it looks exactly like all the other swirling in the room, feels different, feels familiar. This is Iris aswirl, Soph aswirl, himself aswirl, and it doesn't belong on a wall in Visitor's office. These blossoming circles are his family.

Ray holds the sheets to his chest and looks again at the map. A tiny Golden Yolktown is there, and the factory, and even Ray's own abandoned and falling down childhood home. And finally he sees it, the tiny farmhouse in which Iris and Soph are asleep right now. It's farther out from town, more isolated, and deeper into in the dome fields than he fully realized. Clouds drift over the topography and startle him. Apparently, the map is a map of now, a live image, or it's a segment of earlier time. On a rural highway, ant-like far below, a delivery truck makes its way. Another movement catches Ray's eye, but it's not on the map. On the table next to the journal the surface of the tea wisps. The tea tag reads *Give Forgiveness; That is Your Greatness.* A curl of vapor lifts from the tea. It steams. Ray touches Visitor's cup. It's hot. Ray jerks upright. His eyes adjust and focus, and on the other side of the room is Visitor's desk, and next to Visitor's desk is Visitor's office couch, and sitting on the coach, legs crossed, looking amused, is Visitor herself.

"Mr. Egg-o-scope," she says. "I didn't think you had the balls to take the bait."

Ray's hands shake so hard that he drops all three swirling images. He stoops to pick them up but fight or flight adrenaline is kicking in so hard he can't feel his fingers or unclench his fists.

Visitor uncrosses her long legs and stands up. "Now, now," she says, almost gently. She picks up the sheets. She steers Ray to her office chair and sits him down. She sets the sheets on his lap. She lifts both of his hands, massages them open, and places the teacup between them, cupping his hands in her hands to help him hold it steady. The warmth is soothing, if a little too hot, and so is Visitor's touch. His trembling eases. After a moment he can hold the cup himself without spilling.

Visitor sits back down on the couch, re-crosses her legs. The heels of her boots look like they mean business. "Sip."

Ray sips. The steam feels good against his face. "You left the key on purpose. To trap me? Why?"

"Who's trapping you? You did what you did. I saw opportunity. I like leverage. I have a knack for it. That's how I got to be who I am."

"And who are you?"

"Only and always *Visitor* to you."

"My family—"

"Shh," she says, finger to lips. "I've earned my prize and now I'm deciding how to spend it." She looks at him intensely, as if he is a purchase she is considering. Only a minute or so passes but it feels like forever. "Huh."

"I need help," he says.

"Yes. That is how and why this arrangement works. You want to know what's happening to your wife and daughter, how they became pregnant, if it's safe or dangerous, and what caused it, and if they'll be okay."

Ray nods. "Thank you."

She lets out a truncated half-laugh. "Don't thank me. The same unanswered questions that drive you, drive me. That's how I guessed you might take the key and do something stupid. Now you're the one who is going to do the hard work of finding out for both of us."

"But…how can you not know?"

Another long stare, as if he is a cost-benefit sheet and not a person. He guesses she is assessing various strategies of withholding and sharing information based on her desired outcomes.

"Let me tell you about the origins of this company," she says. "More than two centuries ago. A cheap and modestly profitable drug manufactured to do one thing only partially well ended up doing something wildly unexpected and more valuable extremely well at enormous profit. But someone had to have the foresight to think of luck and long game and put in the investment and imagination to turn the unexpected into the extraordinary—and along the way expose many people to danger and take a few real risks that broke a few actual living, breathing eggs, not just metaphorical ones. Sometimes when just one person takes the time to understand the unknown, they change the course and quality of life for all humanity, and in so doing accumulate enormous amounts of control, which I now benefit from and plan to exert toward the exact same end." She pauses here, as if a full explanation had been given.

Ray shakes his head.

Visitor lets out a breath that sounds like disappointment. "In this case, the domes began exactly as what we all say they are. As Scrubland expanded worldwide, we still needed food. So we invented the high-yield agricultural systems we call domes, but—law of unintended consequences—they have... *evolved*. And in that, I see opportunity. I see a long game and the need for imagination. Others see danger—not without reason—and would snuff the evolving domes out. Others see stupid, short-term gains that could erase something that would change the world, the future, the course of humanity."

"The Civil War," says Ray. "In the internal corporate struggle, you're Mrs. Long Game."

"Ms. Imagination."

"I don't want my family to be the living, breathing broken eggs in whatever omelet—"

"Oh, wow. You haven't grasped yet that you're the canary."

Ray stays quiet and tries to project confidence, like he knows more than he does, or at least that he isn't buying her bluff. But he doesn't have a good poker face. He suspects he's coming off as authentically flabbergasted as he truly is.

"This will be something. Follow me."

Visitor's heel-clicks echo down the hallways as the lights turn on before her and turn off behind her. Ray tucks the swirling sheets inside his jacket, just in case they are useful, though Visitor doesn't seem the type to overlook things that are useful. She pauses at a laboratory door, motions for Ray to wait. She goes in and soon comes back out with one of the shiny bullet cylinders from the pneumatic tube system and hands it to him without explanation. They continue down the hallways, to the reception area, and they cross the skybridge and descend the metal stairs to the factory floor.

•

Visitor flicks a switch that turns on a light at the other end of the factory floor, by the locker room. Not much light, but enough.

She powers on the Egg-o-scope like someone highly familiar with its operation. It hums and whines as it warms up. Then she does what Ray does when he begins his shift every day: She lifts and turns the bolt by the conveyor track that, somewhere behind the wall, in the refrigerated section, engages the track with the specific belt that holds the eggs and feeds them through. She stomps on the pedal with her boot. Moments later, eggs whiz out of one square hole in the wall, the entry hole, fly by the Egg-o-scope at high speed, and whiz back into the other square hole, the exit hole.

"Whoa," says Ray, genuinely disturbed. "You're supposed to actually look at them. You can't just let them fly by. Who knows what's inside them?"

Visitor smiles, genuinely delighted, maybe a little perplexed. "Inside them?" She stomps the floor pedal and the conveyor whines to a halt. She takes an egg from the conveyor and holds it as if to drop it on the floor. She raises an eyebrow. Ray feels equally scared and interested. The egg drops. It doesn't so much crack open on the cement as crumble into a chalky mess. She picks up another, drops it. It also crumbles.

Ray stoops, inspects. It's not even shell, more like some kind of ceramic. "I don't understand."

She starts the conveyor again. The eggs whiz by. Every fifteen seconds or so, there's an empty stretch where two eggs in a row are missing. The same empty stretch appears over and over again.

"Why?" says Ray. If they're not eggs…then. He can't fathom what he's been spending his days doing for so long, all these years.

Visitor runs her hand along the tapered cone of the Egg-o-Scope, "the business end." She grabs it, twists it hard. It doesn't take much to take it off completely. She walks it to Ray, shows him the hollow, empty interior. It's a mere prop. A thin metal shell of nothing.

"What have I been looking at? What have I been doing?"

"Nothing," she says. "You're my canary. You haven't been looking at anything at all. *I've* been looking at *you*. Well, my AI has. You and others like you. The exact right kind of people in the right proximity to domes. To see if the effluence from the domes is really changing you. And guess what?"

It has, Ray thinks. He absentmindedly takes out the swirling sheets, stares into them. Soph is right.

"Yes," she says. "And deeply. Way down in the mitochondrial and eukaryotic process and subprocesses. On the genetic level."

He could murder her right now, bash her head in with the empty metal cone, if she wasn't the only thing between his family and Scrubland, his only lifeline to some kind of understanding, and help, and hope.

"Help us," he says.

"Here's what you're going to do—"

"But I *saw* it," he says, hoping this will change things. "I saw it. An eye flicked open. Yellow. Vertical pupil. I saw colors." He holds up the sheets. "Like these."

She nods. "The AI detected your changes some time ago, and recently they accelerated. That's why I came. I had to launch a more invasive test via what you think of as an Egg-o-Scope. I had to look deeper. I know it hurt. And, really, I'm sorry for that."

"But what did I see?"

"What do you see when you dream, when you have a nightmare? Some image made out of emotions and internal fears. Whatever makes you *you*. What did Ebenezer say to the ghost of Marley? *You may be an undigested bit of beef, a blot of mustard, a crumb of cheese, a fragment of underdone potato.* Like that."

Ray has no idea why the hell she's talking about potatoes. "But the swirl of colors?"

"That is interesting," she says. She removes a yellow Moleskine from her pocket. She must have a stockpile of them. She jots in her black swirl of ink. When she's done, she looks at him again in that coldly assessing way of hers. "Here's what you're going to do. Keep the key. Take it to a dome. Go inside. Examine. Inspect. I want you to place something alive in the cylinder, animal or vegetable, doesn't matter. Bring it back to me. Report everything in detail. This is the fastest way to get me the information I need. You help me, I help you."

"Why can't you just go yourself?" Rays suspects an opportunity here, his own leverage, but he can't fully locate it.

"I'm being watched in ways that you aren't. But it won't be long before they know about you. I'm a half-step ahead of the others for a split second. We have a window. The key I gave you is buried a few layers deep in the system. For now. Trust me when I tell you that you'll get a better deal with me than with my counterparts."

"*Counterparts*? If there are no eggs, then what about chickens? No Chicken Shit? You said *effluence*? What's in the domes? What am I getting into?"

"Nothing you're not balls deep in already. Go in. Look around. Hang around. I need your eyes and ears. Fill the cylinder. Report."

"So, I'm on the checkered board now. Not a butt louse. I'm the queen's actual pawn."

"You're a good knight, Roy," she says.

"It's Ray. A knight? How so?"

"*Goodnight*, Ray. You know what to do."

•

Less than an hour later, Ray sits in a lawn chair on the little square of cracked cement that is their back patio. It must be nearly midnight. He doesn't want to wake Iris and Soph. Adrenaline still courses through him, clouding his mind, and he's not sure what, if anything, he's discovered. Under his shirt, the polychromatic sheets spin and billow. Out in the fields, the moon glimmers down on the grass, which bends and ripples in the wind. Ray imagines fingers of air writing messages on the sod. If he can focus and decipher them, everything will make sense.

The glass patio door slides open. Iris, with a beer. "Can't sleep?" she says. She pulls up a rickety lawn chair, sets the bottle, beading with condensation, on his knee.

"Drink for me," she says.

Ray takes a sip. The carbonation fizzes in his mouth. It feels exactly right.

"We need to talk," he says.

"I don't remember us having sex either," she says. "Not since the promotion when I started doing more births. I thought we'd talk about it soon. I don't know what happened, but I talked to some other doulas. And they say it happens all the time. You see woman after woman birthing, laboring, and it's beautiful and natural, but your body is like: *Fuck you.* It says: *Not me.* Your hormones react and your libido just, you know, fizzes out."

"Fizzes out," says Ray, and sips the beer.

"But here we are, and I don't know. I mean, did we do it in our sleep? Did we have sleep sex while dreaming and don't remember?"

Ray looks at her. "I don't know." They laugh a little—or at least start to, and then they both get quiet again. The wind is whipping and roaring way out across the fields, but here in their backyard everything is perfectly still. Ray rips a little shred off the beer label and it flutters down to his feet. There's no wind here at all.

"Do you want a paternity test?" she says. "I'd be okay with it. We need some kind of test, don't we?"

"I don't want a paternity test," he says. "Well, maybe I do. Maybe we need all the tests they have, but there's something else. There's something more I have to tell you. Soph and I both have secrets, and I—"

"I'm listening," says Soph.

Startled, Ray and Iris turn around in their seats. Soph is poking her head out the sliding-glass door. She's good at creeping around the house without them hearing. She's always been like this since she was little, a tiny cookie ninja tiptoeing from bedroom to kitchen to sneak snacks and ice cream in the middle of the night.

"I'll tell her, Dad," she says. Soph pulls up a lawn chair, the one with the fist-sized hole in the webbing. There's a long, quiet moment, and then Soph takes a deep breath and says it, the whole thing, the pregnancy, the no sex, the appointment with Dr. Z. Gupta, and her abortion already on the calendar. And the apple. "Look at the fields," she says. "Look at the domes. Tell me they're not affecting us. These things always affect people like us."

Iris is struggling to be calm. She leans forward. She presses her palms together. "Soph," she says.

Ray thinks she's about to ask Soph to tell the truth, to admit she's lying, but Ray interrupts.

"I have my own thing," he says. "Can I tell my thing?"

"Ray," says Iris, giving him a sharp look in the eye. "We already have a thing. We can't do another thing."

Soph stays silent a moment, likely sensing—as Ray senses—that her mom is on the verge of losing it. Soph looks at Ray. "Where did you go tonight, Dad? I saw you roll the Toyota down the driveway."

Iris looks at him, eyes wide.

"I have a thing," he says. He holds up the metal cylinder Visitor gave him, as a kind of physical symbol of the whole thing. "And it sort of explains all the other things. Or it could."

Iris nods. "Take a drink for me," she says. "In fact, finish it. I'm getting you a second beer."

A moment later, second beer in hand, Ray begins telling his thing: "There was an anomaly."

"There are never anomalies," says Iris.

"Well—that's also kind of true. Truer than I thought. Anyway,

I flinched," he says. "I hit the red button. I thumb-triggered in for a look." He tells the rest of his thing. The break-in. Getting caught. The truth about the Egg-o-Scope and Visitor's mission. He displays the cylinder again. All of it. He takes the sheets from under his shirt, gives each to its rightful owner. "So, you tell me," he says. "What do we do?"

They all sit in their lawn chairs not exactly believing each other, but not disbelieving either. They watch the sheets billow and surge. Soph hands hers back to Ray. "I don't want it," she says.

Iris gets up and goes to the kitchen. When she comes back she has a third beer in hand. "Obviously, we can't take her at face value, can't trust her." She twists off the cap, hands the beer to Ray. "Honey, you're getting a little drunk tonight," she says.

Ray is okay with this. He sips the beer. They all hug their bodies in the night chill and watch the wind ripple the fields, the moon glow bone-white on the distant egg domes. They do this for a long time, looking out. Ray feels buzzed. He imagines the domes as the swollen bellies of pregnant women protruding up through the grass.

"So, what's inside of them?" says Soph. "The domes. Does anybody really know?"

"Do I do what she asks?" says Ray. "Do I go?" He takes the bunny key from his pocket, holds it up.

"Seems like it's that or Scrubland," says Iris. "Or the Shit at a minimum—or the effluence, or whatever it is now."

"And maybe answers," says Soph. "I'm going with you."

Ray is about to shoot that idea down, but Iris interrupts him. "So am I," she says.

Ray looks at her wide-eyed, shocked that she'd propose risking herself, her daughter, her pregnancy.

"What are they going to do to us that they haven't?" says Iris. "Infect us? Fertilize us?"

"There could be worse things," he says.

"You can't win this argument, Dad," says Soph. "It's our right to see what did this to us, to assume whatever risk we want."

They all three look at each other, and in the almost telepathic way of families who have all lived under the same roof for so long, they agree on what to do next.

•

The RV rolls across the grass slowly, clanking and clattering, and then picks up speed. They're driving through the fields. All three look out the big windshield, at the egg domes looming in the distance. Visitor's medallion and cylinder rattle together loudly in the cup holder. Iris picks up the key, looks at it quizzically.

"Tadpole," says Soph.

"Bunny-like yin-yang," says Ray.

"Sperm," says Iris. She doesn't say it angrily, but when Ray side-glances to look at her, she looks angry, staring down at the key in her hand. She places the medallion back in the cup holder where it rattles against the cylinder over the next half hour, like a constant reminder, like a war drum. The nearest dome gets bigger and bigger and fills the entire windshield, and then Ray turns off the vehicle at the bottom of a grassy embankment that leads up to the door. They sit together in silence, listening to gusts of wind against the side of the RV. The wind-bursts quicken the pulse of anger in Ray's veins.

"It's time," says Soph.

"Evidence," says Iris. "We need to get in, document, get out." She presses record on her phone, states her name, the date and time, and starts describing their mission and what has happened to them while she walks up the hill to the dome.

As a last-minute thought, Ray rummages through the back of the RV, digging through the camping and fishing equipment that Iris's father left carefully stowed there when he passed away. Ray doesn't know what he needs. He chooses a pack, not sure what it contains, and he jogs up the hill to catch up with his family.

At the top of the embankment, Ray stands next to Iris and Soph, who stand in front of what must be the entrance, a big door maybe thirty feet wide and thirty feet tall, with a seam in the middle where it looks like it will part and slide open. Iris opens a plastic lid next to the door, beneath which is a reader with a shape identical to the medallion. Soph places it—the bunny, the fat comma, the whatever-it-is—against the reader. A light blinks.

"Stay behind me," says Ray, but they don't. They stand in front of him.

There's a popping sound. Several hissing air blasts. The two halves of the door slide apart slowly, the teeth unlocking. Ahead of them is a short tunnel, a ramp that descends to a second door, a circular portal of elliptically overlapping plates. The airlock is fiercely illuminated with blue light. It blinks on and off at long intervals. Three abreast, they march down to the other end, phones at the ready. At the second door Soph again places the medallion. Behind them, the teeth of the first door engage, clank together, and tighten. Air hisses and pops in the chamber. Ray feels pressure build in his ears. He feels woozy, lightheaded. The blue lights blink rapidly and then turn off altogether, leaving them in darkness. The second, circular door dilates open with a whoosh. They stand close together in darkness. They put their phones in flashlight mode. They step through.

They stumble through tall ferns. They touch the trunks of giant trees. It's like they haven't entered anything at all but have instead exited into a deep, expansive forest. The air is humid and smells of earth. Breathing feels lighter and easier. Ray's mind feels clearer, senses heightened. Insect wings whir and hum. They wander through tall trees until they come upon a clearing, a mound covered in thick moss.

"Huddle," he whispers. "Family huddle."

Before they can huddle, though, they all spot it through

the trees: a lake, moonlight rippling the surface. They walk to it through the woods until they all stand together on a beach of smooth pebbles. They turn off their flashlights. The moon is bright. There appears to be an island near the other end, maybe a half-mile distant, aswirl in mist. They look out across the water and listen to wavelets lapping the shore. A fish jumps.

"It's beautiful," says Iris. She doesn't need to say it, but Ray is glad she does. An owl hoots. Trees rim the moonlit lake, casting tree-shaped shadows across the water. Beyond the far shore, the land rises into a ridge. The family stands agape, not knowing what to do. They skip rocks, stare up at a star-filled sky, and listen to night calls. Ray came for the yellow eye, but its opposite, the silver orb of moon, shimmers down on the water.

"I'm confused," says Soph after a long stretch of quiet. "I don't even know if this is real or not. Are we inside or outside?"

"Keep watch," says Iris. "Be alert." She scans with her phone, recording, but Ray can see that it looks murky on her screen in the low light. Maybe an expert could lighten it up later.

A succession of droplets—melodic drips, languorous plinks and plops—chime from the island, across the water, like rain beads spilling from leaf to puddle, but more resonant, as if falling through metal pipes or into a cavern pool. The scattered sequence of liquid notes resounds, is silent for long intervals, and sounds again. The family sits down together on the pebbly beach and listens to the rippling pulse of wavelets, the island's intermittent drip-drops, and the chirps, croaks, flutters, and splashes of living things.

Then, by some invisible signal, they all stand up together, wipe their butts clean of pebbles, and trudge their way through the primordial trees, back to the RV in the sod fields. They look at each other's faces.

"What do we do?" says Ray. The dome reflects pale moonlight through the RV windshield.

"We didn't fill up the cylinder," says Iris.

"At the very least, we have to go back in and grab a fern or tear some lichen off a tree, or something," says Soph.

Ray didn't forget at all. He knew he should fill the cylinder. Would've taken but a minute. He suspects Soph and Iris also thought about it, but no one said anything. Why? Because they didn't want to leave—or, in any case, they all want a reason to come right back. Why? Part of Ray resists the answer: the inside of the dome felt better than anything they've ever known outside.

Acknowledging this feels…topsy turvy. The place they were sure was the enemy, the culprit was…well, they still didn't know what it was. Right now it was just a feeling, or instinct, caused by trees, moonlight on water, melodic dripping, and the smell of rich soil. Who knew if you could trust such things?

"We all want to stay, so let's just stay," says Ray. "I don't know if it's smart or foolish, dangerous or not, but…we agreed to observe. The longer we stay, the more we see. And it must be after 1 a.m. So, we could camp out…" He shrugs.

Enough said. The family moves into logistical mode, rooting through the back of the RV, through Iris's father's old camping supplies, which appear to cover all the basics. The food situation isn't great, but the old man stowed a bundle of those military-grade meals and drinks in pouches that are supposed to get you through an apocalypse, so no one is going to perish on that front.

Ray starts the RV and they drive up the grassy embankment, down the blinking tunnel, through the elliptical dome door, and into the mossy forest, where they slowly navigate around giant trees and crunch over ferns until the beach pebbles pop under the tires.

They unload Iris's father's dusty old supplies and pitch camp. For a late-night snack, they follow the directions on the apocalypse food, boiling lake water then plopping the packets in to warm them up. Fog undulates and churns across the lake. The island tolls out a chain of drips and drops. They all look and listen. A misty gauze wafts up the beach. The sit in silence around the fire and eat the almost-lasagna.

While they eat, something out on the lake—a few some-things—paddle in closer to shore, bobbing on the wavelets just be-yond the glow of the firelight on water. "Hey," Ray whispers and points, but he doesn't need to. Soph and Iris are staring as well, a little apprehensive. The creatures spin to paddle away and drift into the light for just a moment. Geese, maybe? Or a kind of goose. The head isn't shaped right: bigger, blockier. They're all so jet black it's like they absorb the light around them. Then they're gone.

"Night geese?" Ray whispers.

"We don't have a name for whatever those are," says Soph. "Look up."

There are quadruple the usual number of stars in the sky.

"Not our sky," says Iris. "Not even a little bit."

They replace the boiled lake water in the pot with water from one of the big apocalypse pouches. When warm, they mix in cocoa and sip. It's good, despite the "lasts forever" flavor. The end-of-the-world marshmallow product is rock hard in its suctioned-tight packet. Soph tears the bag open and works at chipping a marsh-mallow off the slowly expanding mass to roast over the fire.

"Are we going to talk about how we know so much less now that we're here?" says Soph. "It's like our investigation went in reverse."

"I'm trying to grapple," says Ray. "I've spent more than a de-cade believing these domes were giant chicken coops."

"I wouldn't hold your breath for answers," says Iris. "Golden Yolk lost control of what they made. So, we're on our own. The answer is: what's best for us?"

"What's weird is that I feel a little better," says Soph. "I mean, I'm getting a fucking abortion ASAP, so…yeah. But I came in here wanting to point a finger at someone and then kick that someone in the teeth for what they did to me, but…" She's quiet for a mo-ment. "The sound of lake water lapping against a pebbly shore?

Night geese? This is the closest I've ever been to nature, and I don't know how to blame the entirety of nature and all its fucked-up strange evolving. It's like blaming existence for existence."

"But Golden Yolk?" says Ray.

"Oh, I will kick their teeth in," says Soph. "They're to blame for making a total fucking hellhole of the whole world. But it's like they accidently, despite themselves, catalyzed a better world into existence, or found a portal, or...." She shrugs. "I've never liked something as much in my life as sitting in this forest under stars, listening to weird water drips. It's like I knew the *concept* of forest, but..." She shakes her head. She's given up on separating a petrified marshmallow and instead pokes her roasting stick into the fire. A log shifts. A spray of embers sparkle and fade.

"There's nothing to be done," says Iris, "so the thing to do is get back to normal as fast as we can. Visitor seems to be on our side, or at least willing to work with us. Dad isn't going out to the poop station as far as we can tell. Nothing needs to change. I'll have the baby—"

"Whoa," says Soph. "*Mom.* You just said like ten crazy things in a row."

Iris's eyes widen, shining with firelight. "And you just monologued incoherently about lake water and the existence of existence."

"We're all out of sorts," says Ray. He instantly regrets it when both wife and daughter look at him with a snarl. He is aware that this is one of those times when he needs to just shut up, but he can't stop him himself. Some part of him insists on leaning in. "We're all tired. So many confusing things. Night geese. Crazy stars. We've got to give each other some space, some generosity."

"Well, Dad," says Soph, "Mom wants you to spend the rest of your life sitting at a machine pretending to see eggs while AI has its way with you, probing all your thoughts, memories, and feelings so it can clone you for the future submissive slave army. Or whatever it's really doing. You'll never know the half of it."

"They say I have a special amygdala. An accumbens, and such, and—"

"*Yeah.*" Soph and Iris both chortle at the same time, with dead-on identical sarcasm. Ray hears Iris's mother's voice in it. Funny how things get passed down.

"Your daughter thinks she's going to live off the grid in some kind of mutating forest," says Iris, "where there's no medical care or, as far as we know, viable food source. And what even lives here that could attack us at any moment?"

The fire pops, and the group startles. They go silent for a moment, probably all considering, as Ray is, what could be in these woods, out in the darkness, at this very moment, gnashing its terrible teeth, rolling its terrible eyes, showing its terrible claws. The island drips a single loud drip.

"I'm not saying it would be easy," said Soph. "Supplies and skill would be required. But it's how humans used to live, long ago, before we ruined the world. And, TBH? Say there is a tribe of abominable sasquatch yeti out there, ready to rip me apart and chew on my leg—I'll take that risk before going back to live in a Corpo-Agzone with zero future."

"You're lucky for the Corpo," says Iris. "In the Scrub—"

"Speaking of monsters," Soph interrupts, "what's growing in your belly right now, Mom? Do you even know what's going to claw and chew its way out?"

Iris bursts into tears. Sobs.

Soph stares horrified. "Shit," she whispers. "I'm sorry. Too far. I…I'm going to pee."

"Take a flashlight, stay close," says Ray, but Soph ignores him. She leaves without the flashlight. She goes far. She's at the age where she won't do something for the sole reason that her parents asked her to do it. He should've forbidden her to take the flashlight and ordered her to go far away. He watches until he sees her phone light turn on in the trees. She is walking back in the direction of the dome, so at least it's ground they've covered before.

Iris throws a little log on the fire, and a hundred tiny sparks take flight amidst the rising smoke. "I don't know why I'm fighting with her," she says. "I don't mean to. My mom and I did the same thing, and I promised myself—fucking *promised* myself—that I wouldn't do that. And now look at me. Taking all my shit out on her. What the fuck is wrong with me?"

Ray sighs, digging deep. "She loves you. You love each other. That won't change." He picks up Soph's stick and pokes the coals. He decides not to say anything else. But his brain overrides him and it comes out anyway. "You're sure you want to keep it?"

Iris takes a deep breath through her nose with her eyes momentarily closed. Then she bites her lower lip, nods her head *yes*. "It's not that I don't have the same worries as Soph, but—I can't explain this—it just feels right. I feel good inside. Want to hear my craziest thought?"

"I love your crazy thoughts," he says. "They're usually not even half as crazy as mine, but it still makes me feel less alone with all my own stuff."

"My worst fear is that it's some sort of parasitic drug running through me. Like, I've heard that certain parasites can live inside you, excreting a substance that makes you feel great while they feed off you. Like a more intense version of how certain bugs, at least back in the old world, maybe they're still in the Scrubland, would numb your skin before poking you and drinking from a vein. My fear is that this thing inside me is just giving me some kind of happy juice."

"That's…okay. Yeah. Okay. That is pretty dark. And too close to real to dismiss."

"It is and it isn't. You could say the same thing about romantic love and sex—fueled by chemical happy juice that nature gives you to get the job done. Looking in your baby's eyes is a rush of oxytocin. And—"

"But I'm not feeling it," Soph calls out from the trees.

Ray and Iris jolt. Soph steps into the edge of the firelight from the shadows.

"Sorry. Didn't mean to scare you. Didn't really have to pee. Just needed space. But I wanted to chime in to point out that I would probably be feeling the same happy juice, right? But it's like my parasitic thing gave me grouchy, pissed-off juice. So…you know. Maybe you're just actually happy, Mom?"

Ray's confused. Soph sounds almost nice, but there must be a barb in it somewhere. Soph takes her seat by the fire. She has brought back a flat rock and uses it to chip at the mass of marshmallows.

"That's… a good point," says Iris, enunciating a little too slowly word by word, probably carefully choosing what she says to avoid stepping on a Soph landmine. "And I meant to say that I think the way I feel about this pregnancy is not so different than how you feel about this forest. It's hard to explain, but it sits well with my soul. Maybe I'm dumb or overly optimistic, but I'm not going to let reason and common sense cloud my good judgment when there's such a solid gut feeling to lean on."

Soph laughs. "I get you. I was going to make a joke about being an awesome sister to a swamp creature changeling child, hopefully programmed to be a brother, but… too soon?" She saws at the marshmallows with her stone. "I heard about what you said about you and your mom and fighting. And I'm sorry. I don't want to fight. And I know I'd probably die if I tried to live here. I'd last like a month. And I know the corpo-overlords wouldn't even let me. I just…I hate what all the previous generations have made of the world. I *hate* it."

There is a honking sound from above: *honk, honk, honk.* And against the dark blue of star-stuffed night appears a black-black V of geese, or goosish things—even in the dark Ray can see the shapes aren't quite goose enough. *Honk, honk, honk.* They circle the lake. The family hears them splash down in the water, out in the darkness. Drip, drip, drip goes the island.

"I love those guys," whispers Soph. "Night geesishes. And I hate that Golden Yolk owns my whole life and I don't feel like I've even started living it yet. And they invaded my body and knocked me up—or at least angered nature into doing that, like shaking a hornet's nest and throwing it right at my face. Everything is their fault. I hate them forever."

There's silence now. Ray wants to help his daughter, but her anger is directed at something so big it's like saying you're going to go to war against the sky, against the sun. How do you even start?

"They're vulnerable," says Iris.

Of course she's right. Ray feels embarrassed by his—what do they call it?—learned helplessness? It's like he's been corpo-trained all these years to see them as impregnable so that even when their cracks and fissures are right in front of him he's blind to it. "The internal faction?"

"Visitor lady needs us," says Soph.

"For what, though?" says Ray. "We don't understand anything that's happening."

"Neither does she," says Iris. "But she's in a fight. A death match, I bet. She wants things—to survive. She's singled us out as helpful. Maybe crucial."

"We have more power than we think," says Soph. "We need to remember that to get what we want."

A series of slow plips and plops ring out from across the lake, joined halfway through by a kind of plaintive honk.

"Those water sounds," says Soph. "Weird. Maybe my little brother will honk like that when he hatches."

"Please stop, Soph," says Iris. "Show more respect and empathy for my position."

"Sorry," says Soph. She has managed to separate a large glob of marshmallow and spear it to the end of her stick. "I'll try to be a good sister. I'll always wonder. We all will. But I'll tap deep down into my reservoir of love. On that topic…about what one does with a spontaneous pregnancy…do you have empathy and respect for *my* decision?"

"Yes," say Ray and Iris at the same time.

"Thank you," says Soph. She shifts in her seat and looks both surprised by the support and as if she's ready to argue with them no matter what they say. She sticks her marshmallow mass directly into the flames. "I want to tell you something," she says.

Ray and Iris are quiet, expectant. There's a distant splash in the water, a leaping fish, maybe, or frog. The marshmallow looks impervious to fire. Soph rotates the stick.

"I went to a party, just a few months ago. I snuck out of the house after midnight." Here, Soph pauses, gauging what the parental reaction will be. Iris gives a small nod of understanding. Ray finds a spot in the fire to stare at. He watches the heat glide and swirl across the surface of an ember. He doesn't want to interrupt Soph or change her mind.

"I had my eyes on someone, someone I wanted to make out with. I don't usually go to those parties. This was my first time sneaking out. It's not my scene."

Soph takes the marshmallow pile out of the flames and examines its stark white and entirely unchanged appearance, sticks it back in again.

"We went upstairs to the bedroom to make out. We talked a long time, and then she took her shirt off."

"*She?*" says Iris.

"She," says Soph. "And we did all the things. Well, I don't know what *all* the things are, but we did lots of the things."

There's a long silence. Soph looks Ray in the eyes, then Iris, then Ray again. Out in the lake, more splashes.

"Yep. I stuck my hand down her pants—"

"Okay, okay, okay," says Iris, holding up her hands. "We get it."

"Girls can like girls, that's fine," says Ray. This sounds dumb, and he's not sure why he said it. Even more, he's not sure why he's already thought of this scenario and planned things he might say. On some level, he's always known, and in stray thoughts about his daughter always wanted to tell her it was fine, it would all be okay.

"I'm not even sure if I'm, like, a lesbian or what," says Soph. "I don't want to overthink it right now, label myself, box myself in. What I do know is that I've only ever imagined making out with girls. Even at age five, when they kiss at the end of, like, a really old Disney movie, I always imagined myself as the prince."

Soph examines her stick again. The stuff isn't indestructible, after all. It's getting gooey, and the underside has skipped brown and gone straight to black. She blows on it, and part of it glows red. She sticks it right back into the coals. Apparently, her plan is to destroy it rather than eat it.

"So, this girl, she told me I wasn't allowed to talk to her at school. That we can still be friends, but no interaction in public. She has a boyfriend now too. Total douchebag. She's overcompensating. As a way to deny and purge me." Soph lets the marshmallow slide off into the fire. She looks at her mom.

Iris stands up and sits next to Soph. She knows exactly what to do and wraps her arms around her daughter. Soph nestles in.

"I didn't want to tell you," says Soph. "I had to tell an incriminating truth so that you'd believe I wasn't lying about the other thing." The melty marshmallow puddle finally catches flame, rapidly blackens to ash, and crumbles into the fire. "I believe you both," she says. "I believe Dad's whole experience with the egg and the mean lady. I believe Mom's pregnancy is inexplicable, even if I hate to think about it because, you know, gross. I believe you both because I know what has happened to me." The island drips three bell-like drips.

"Thank you for telling us," says Iris. "What we all need is trust."

"I have an appointment Monday," says Soph. "I need you both to pick me up before my last class. To have an abortion."

Black shapes slide out of the water, run across the pebbly beach, and into the foggy woods. *Inky* is exactly the right word for them, the way their movements look wet and fluid on land. They all stare for several minutes. Soph whispers to Iris, so quiet Ray can't hear it. Iris rubs Soph's back without saying anything. Sonorous droplets reverberate through the mist.

"I want to get out to the island and understand those sounds," says Ray. "They're strange, but beautiful. I want to see what makes them."

Soph and Iris nod in agreement.

"I wonder if I could swim out to it, maybe from the opposite shore, so I could walk around and explore," says Ray. As soon as the idea is out of his mouth, Ray thinks of the dark water, unknown creatures swimming below his legs.

"So, you're the one who gets eaten by the lake monster, Dad. Good to know," says Soph.

"Next time we'll bring my dad's old canoe," says Iris. "It's in the barn somewhere."

Next time. Ray likes the sound of this.

In the ten minutes before they go to bed, there is a quiet stretch in which they are all thinking. Ray imagines Iris and Soph are thinking about what's going to happen next, how to manage Visitor, play this game of chess with her, and get whatever it is they all want. He doesn't think any of them know exactly what they want, but if he has to guess? Soph wants, aside from an abortion, the world to be different than what it is, more fair, more natural and beautiful, less predetermined—and to strike back with merciless revenge at Golden Yolk and cause some real damage. Iris wants the fulfillment and joy of the baby (or whatever it might be), which at its core is what? What is the core feeling and yearning of nurturing a life into being and caring for it? He can't pinpoint a word for it, but he can grasp the feeling.

What is embarrassing is that he isn't sure what *he* wants. Even after they all say goodnight, he lays in his musty old sleeping bag, wavelets lapping. Occasional mysterious drips and plinks are dripping and plinking out on the lake. Night geese paddling about. He can only come up with absences: not-danger, not-worry, not-anxiety. So, he guesses he must want the opposite, even though it doesn't feel very ambitious: safety, calm, quiet. What he pictures in his mind is holding a cup of coffee in the morning at their campfire, mist wafting off the lake, Soph and Iris sitting nearby too tired to talk yet, and all of them enjoying the silence and the company of each other with no pressures, no hurry. A canoe waiting to glide across the water. Whatever you call *that*—that's what he wants.

A weird thought pops into mind. He barely knew his own grandfather—the man had started out a farmer back when the old farms were rapidly dying out. They said he'd been good with wood, back when it was plentiful enough that anyone could buy it at stores that sold it. Made chairs. Tables. Planted seeds and watched them grow. Ray imagines himself doing these things—old, ancient, satisfying things—and these visions become the stuff of dreams.

•

They sleep in a little after the long night, and when they drive the RV out of the dome airlock Saturday morning, they are greeted by a strange sight: what appears to be a fully suited-up, dead astronaut lying on the grass next to an ambulance. They get out to inspect. The airlock pops and hisses behind them, lacing its interlocking teeth tight together as it cinches shut. The astronaut's face mask reflects clouds and sky. Ray nudges the spaceperson with his toes, and he sits up—Dr. Z. Gupta.

"Oh, my goodness," says the doctor, his voice muffled inside the suit. "I waited all night. Fell asleep. Do you have her sample?"

Ray gives him the canister, stuffed with a fern and a handful of moss they'd grabbed at the last minute. The doctor holds it like it's a rare artifact, secures it somewhere in the ambulance, which apparently he drove across the fields himself.

"If you don't mind," he said. "I'd like to examine you all." He nods to Iris. "Check the baby. Take some blood samples."

Ray and Iris permit it. They want to know the baby is okay, want any answers he might have. So, they let the doctor fill vials with their blood. He peppers them with questions about what they saw inside and jots a few notes. He extends a tube from the back of the ambulance, with a fitting on the end that fits snugly against Iris's belly. On a small screen, it produces the familiar swirl of colors and dancing halos. "Excellent," says the doctor. "Excellent."

The doctor turns to Soph, who gives him such a clear *fuck you* glare that the man startles.

"Abortion," says Soph. "Now."

"It's Saturday," says Dr. Gupta. "You're scheduled for—"

"Oh, but you're out here on a weekend morning in the sod fields, asleep in a spacesuit on the grass," says Soph. "She's got something on you. Visitor lady. Doesn't she? Promised you something. Threatened you with something. Well—"

"Yes," says the doctor, sighing. "Yes. I need to call in a nurse. Meet me at the facility in—"

There's a terrible sound in the distance. It's akin to a *whump*, but a kind of whump Ray has never heard before. One of the domes in the distance is entirely gone. And around it a line in the grass. A rippling. Coming at them.

"Down, down, down," shouts the doctor. Ray and Soph lay flat. But even as the doctor says this, he doesn't get down himself. With amazing speed, he seatbelts Iris into the seat in the rear of the ambulance, where a paramedic would sit.

Then the wave of air pressure hits them. Soph rolls with it a few feet. Ray rolls with it. The ambulance rocks hard. The doctor is knocked off the rear of the vehicle, onto to his ass, and somersaults backward three or four times, a good fifteen feet. Ray rushes to Iris.

"I'm okay," she says. "I'm okay."

The doctor groans on the grass. Ray helps him to his feet.

"I'll be all right," says the man. "A little sore and bruised to-morrow. That's all."

"They killed it," says Soph, looking in the distance where one of the domes used to be, a few miles away.

"It's her counterparts," says Dr. Z. Gupta. "Visitor wants to preserve the domes. Her rivals see liability, what with the effluence and…" He gestures to Iris and Soph. "I hear they call it *flattening*. A kind of implosion. Apparently extremely complex."

"It's what they're good at," says Soph. "They destroy worlds. It's what they know."

·

Late afternoon, Iris is knocking on the Toyota window. Soph is done. A nurse wheels Soph out to the car, parked at the curb of the medical facility, where Ray has been waiting. He didn't know what to do with himself after he dropped the two off, so he went and bought food, lots of food. He didn't think Soph would want it. Not right away. But just in case. He stocked the fridge with her ice cream. Made mac and cheese. Bought a box of those bars Soph likes. He moved the TV to her bedroom and got some of her favorite comedies ready to watch. He didn't know what else to do, so then he made a basket of bottled water, juice, and snacks for the back seat, pulled up to the curb of the medical center, put on some calming classical music, and fell asleep with his head against the window until just now, when Iris knocked.

Soph rolls her eyes when Ray gets out of the car, which is meant to show that she finds the nurse and wheelchair ridiculous and unnecessary. What Ray sees, though, is that Soph is uncomfortable and in pain, and he's glad for the wheelchair. A hot pad, he thinks. He should've brought a hot pad. Ray opens the back door. While Soph gets in, he and Iris stand there in ineffective half crouches, arms spread wide, palms open, ready to catch her. But there's nothing to do. Soph buckles herself. "Let's go," she says. "I want to sleep forever." They're all exhausted after the long night, all in bed by eight.

•

Late Sunday morning, Ray wakes up to a note from Iris, who has snuck out of the house to coach a birth. He peeks in on Soph, watches to make sure she inhales and exhales, waits a little longer until she stirs in her sleep. With a cup of coffee, he crosses the backyard of weeds and sticks. Across the sod fields, blades of grass shimmer in the wind. On Sunday mornings Ray likes to stand out on the edge of the grass to survey the endless green, the horizons. The open space feels like possibility. The immensity of it makes Ray's worries feel reassuringly small—only a few more little blades of grass under the sky. He lifts his mug to his lips. He surveys.

What Ray sees makes him lower his coffee without drinking: little white flowers, by the thousands or millions, bunched together in tight, puffy clusters, like clouds that have drifted onto the ground to rest. Ray has never seen this before. He doubts this is supposed to happen. There are a few dozen of these cumulus flower-heaps between Ray and the horizon. The small ones are house-sized, the big ones larger than a football field. Ray walks out to investigate.

At the edge of the nearest billow, a few hundred yards out, Ray inspects a single bud up close. It's not like any flower he's ever seen; in the center, surrounded by tiny petals, is a perfectly round ball of fluff. He barely grazes it and the petals and ball fall right off. The petals flutter away. The ball sticks to his finger. He holds it up. The delicate white gob wisps in the air then lifts skyward, fairy-like, dropping and rising. Within a few seconds it has diminished into nothing, fizzed out, dispersed.

Ray scans the fields again. There's not a single flower growing by itself. They're all packed in tightly together, each billowing cluster a perfect white island on the grass. Every so often a ball detaches from its patch, wanders skyward, and dissipates into the air. Seeds. Ray looks back at his own lawn. He didn't see them before, but there they are, three white shapes, two palm-sized, one plate-sized.

Ray rounds the house, and in the front yard a single thick, oval cloud encircles the apple tree. He doesn't want to think of this mass as egg-like, but it is darn ovoid, and Ray would know. The aberrant apple has also returned, in miniature form, with a few dozen siblings. Ray gets as close as he can to the tree without stepping on the fluff heap. The apples are the size of cherries, bloodred.

Ray feels dizzy. He sits on the cold cement of the back patio. Inside, Soph is recovering from an abortion, and here outside are clouds of what may have caused all her pain and suffering. He can't let it happen again. His instinct is to carry Soph to the RV, drive her to the closest safe place—the lake in the dome is the image that comes to mind—and then come back and burn everything down, the house, the apple trees, the fields, Golden Yolk itself, everything. He knows he's in a panic and overreacting, but this is also an emergency. The flowers, the fluff balls, the apples: he doesn't understand it, but he knows it's a danger, a crisis.

Ray gets a beer from the fridge and sits back down on the cement. He grips the cold bottle to keep his hands from trembling. He texts Iris *come home*, even though he knows she can't leave a birth, won't have her phone on. He leaves a voicemail for Bob, describing what he's seen—when he's done he feels like maybe calling Bob was impulsive. A mistake. But he needs a friend. A lifeline. Anyone at all.

He finishes the beer quickly, then goes to the barn, where the antique tractor and other old, restored things from earlier generations are piled under tarps. He digs out his deceased father-in-law's

shop vac, an industrial-grade vacuum meant for old-timey renova-
tion work. It has a filter that won't blow lead paint dust back into
the air. Ray hooks up an extension cord and vacuums up the small
clouds in the backyard first. It's a temporary fix, or a visual fix,
or no fix at all. He doesn't want Iris and Soph to see these things
and worry and feel the helpless panic he feels—not until he can
think of a solution. Halfway through the ovoid front yard cloud
the shop-vac whines and screams, stuffed full of fuzz. Ray takes the
vac to the edge of the yard, downwind from the house, places a
trash bag over the canister, and begins shaking the wispy contents
into the bag as carefully as he can.

He's still trying to jiggle fuzz into the bag when he hears a car
door slam. Iris is home. She stands in the front yard and stares
at the remaining half-egg of flowers, at the tiny bloodred apples.
Soph, who must have heard the pop and crackle of tires on the
gravel drive, opens the front door, rubbing sleep from her eyes.

"No no no!" says Ray. "Hey!" He waves an arm to get their attention. He runs toward them but steps on the bag, trips over the
canister, and falls. He lands on the bag and a white burst of cloud
fluff billows over his face. It's in his mouth and nose and eyes. He
lifts himself from the grass, wipes at his face with his arm. Soph
and Iris run toward him. "Get inside!" he yells. They don't listen.
They're still coming to help him. "Seeds!" he yells.

They stop. They grab each other. They run for the house.

Ray washes his face at the outside spigot and vacuums the
rest of the front yard. With a ladder, he picks every tiny, bloodred
apple from the tree and seals them in a trash bag. He strips off his
clothes, puts them in the trash, and hoses himself off on the back
patio. Out in the fields, fluffy white balls drift into the air, one after
another after another. Inside, he goes straight for the shower. With
hot water running over his back, he cups his testicles. They ache.
They feel swollen. He probably banged himself when he fell over
the canister on the lawn. He could also be imagining it—a psycho-

somatic response to inhaling a faceful of the seeds. Or they could be affecting him too, like he suspects they have Iris and Soph.

Showered and dressed, Ray knocks on Soph's door. It sounds like she's running a hairdryer inside. He knocks again loudly and the blowing stops.

"Are you contaminated?" says Soph from the other side.

"Hosed and showered," he says.

Soph opens the door with a sucking sound. The frame is sticky with duct tape, and when Ray's inside she reseals it. They have the HEPA filter on that Soph uses when her summer hay fever kicks in, when the Scrubland weeds blow across the Corpo-Agzone. Soph blow-dries the plastic sheeting that Ray intended, several winters ago, to put on drafty farmhouse windows. It uncrinkles and tightens until it's nearly invisible.

Iris holds up a finger for silence. She dials the phone. Even though it's midday Sunday, Iris is still able to get several former clients on the phone. Apparently, if you guide a woman through the birth of her child she'll pick up when you call.

Iris's phone skills dazzle Ray, who has always hated the dis-embodied-voice feeling of the telephone. He gets immediately tongue-tied and stuttery. Iris is persuasive, calm, confident: There's an emergency; it's agricultural; seeds. Just listening to her, Ray finds himself persuaded of the threat and hopeful others will be-lieve. Call after call, though, the results aren't good. After all, it comes down to eggs, flowering sod fields, and apples. One of Iris's former clients, a legal counsel for Golden Yolktown, recommends an allergist, or a therapist, as well as an infinite source of wealth and power and a taste for Scrubland exile if you're going to try and accuse the Corpo-Agzone of anything through an official channel. All the women she calls are nice, they all say: "I'll see what I can find out and get back to you."

"No one will call back," says Iris. "They think I've lost it. Or they're too scared."

The family sits together on Soph's bed. The HEPA filter whirs. Soph is staring at nothing.

"We're all alone with it," says Iris.

"I refuse to live in this world," says Soph.

Iris places a hand on her lower back, then on her belly. She looks sick to her stomach. A single ball of fluff wafts by Ray, right in front of his nose. He swipes at it, cross-eyed. A gust blows against the house. The plastic sheeting trembles.

"Mom," Soph says.

The way she says it makes Ray's heart speed up. There's a trickle of bright red blood running down Iris's leg.

"Mom," says Soph again.

Iris looks at it. Her face is calm, the affectless kind of calm that is her response to emergencies. "I need the midwives," she says. "And Dr. Z. Gupta."

•

The nurse-midwives arrive first, standing shoulder to shoulder on the farmhouse porch when Ray opens the door. Whenever Ray and Iris gossip about them, they call them Rock, Bird, and Toad, ostensibly because two of them have similar names that are easy to mix up, but also because the descriptions are apt. The women don't wait for an invitation. They rush past him, up the stairs. Ray tries to follow them into the primary bedroom, but they shoo him away. Minutes later, there's faint music, chimes and bells, from the bedroom. A smell like sage. Ray doesn't know if this is a miscarriage, a birth, or something else. Has no choice but to wait.

He looks around for Soph, for company. Her bedroom door is closed, so he places an ear against it and hears her filter-fan and something on the TV, probably one of the movies she's been playing on repeat. White noise to help her sleep. She's still recovering from yesterday's procedure. He can hear the plastic sheeting on her windows crinkling. He wants to knock, doesn't want to be alone, but it feels selfish. Let the kid rest.

He puts on the old work mask he wore when he refinished the living room floor years ago, and he goes to stand at the edge of the western sod fields. Distant storm clouds blow in from the western Scrubland. His testicles either hurt a lot or not at all, but the fact that the feeling only comes when he thinks about the seeds and Iris and Soph probably means it's all in his head, like the bad egg, the yellow eye that flicked open. The sky begins to darken. He can't fight seeds. Not with all the filters in the world. He takes off his mask, breathes in the fresher-feeling Scrubland air.

There's a distant, strange humming that he at first takes to be Soph's filter from inside the house, but it's actually coming from far away. He rounds the house and looks over the sod fields to the east. Evidently, someone from Golden Yolk feels differently about fighting the puffballs. Giant white tents have been erected over the flower patches. Little drones ascend and descend, like bees in and out of a hive. The storm brings more darkness. The tents glow brightly from within.

Whump. Ray doesn't see it happen, but he assumes one of the dozens of domes on the horizon is no longer there. Flattened. He replaces his face mask and braces himself. He sees the ripple race across the grass. It hits the most distant white tent, scattering a swarm of drones and sending a mist of seed-puffs into the air, but the tent holds, and the tents closer to the farmhouse only billow. By the time it reaches Ray, the ripple has lost enough energy from the distance, or from the counter-winds of the storm, that he can barely feel it.

There's a shout from behind him. Dr. Z. Gupta calls to him from the back patio door.

•

They talk in the kitchen. The doctor has already been upstairs. The sturdy midwives carry heavy-looking, high-tech equipment up to the master bedroom. Rain falls, pattering on the roof.

"You should know that Visitor supplied the equipment," says the doctor. "She said to do whatever it takes to help Iris and the baby."

"Can you? Is she in danger?"

"Stop talking and help," says one of the nurse-midwives. Bird. Her look says that of course Iris is in danger, so stop fucking around.

"We'll know more soon," says the doctor. He lugs a bag of supplies up the stairs.

The woman nods her chin to some kind of metal box with dials and switches. It's so heavy, Ray can only lift it one step at a time. When he gets to the top of the stairs, he is hoping to see Iris, but one of the other midwives—Rock—gives him a look that makes it clear he'd be in the way, so he leaves the box where her chin indicates, in the hall. If it were just Dr. Z. Gupta and one his nurses, nothing could keep Ray away. But these ladies have faced pain and death and grief and weathered all sorts of hardship with Iris over the years. She trusts them. He lets them work.

It's early evening. The sun is getting low in the sky, but with the storm clouds it almost looks like night outside. He tries to wait it out in the kitchen, but he can't stand to be alone anymore, so he tiptoes back up the stairs to see if Soph is awake, stepping from long-gone star to long-gone star. Performing the movements, the sequence of steps he performed so many times, brings the flood of memories back like clockwork. Soph's infant cry in the night. Her baby laugh. The sound she'd make sucking a bottle. The first time she baked cookies herself, age seven, and gave him one, a little burnt on the bottom. He can still taste it. He pushes the duct-taped door open.

The absence of Soph in the room disorients him for a moment. Rainfall intensifies on the roof. The wind has picked up. There is a note on her pillow. His heart beats wildly, and his eyes have trouble reading it, but he catches the essence: *In the dome...*

before they destroy it...can't live here anymore...can't let it happen again...I love you...I'll be okay.

He runs to the living room picture window. How did he not see the RV is gone? When did she leave? He considers chasing her down in the Toyota, but there's not even a glimpse of her on the horizon. She probably left hours ago, before the nurse-midwives arrived. She has the bunny medallion, the key, and he has nothing. He'd only arrive at a closed airlock door, no way to get in. Meanwhile, Iris's life may be in danger. There's nothing to do but stand and look out the window.

Lightning flashes. Thunder. Out on the sod, dozens of white tents glow like lanterns.

•

Other than meeting the women halfway up the stairs when they call for food and water, Ray stays on the first floor and the midwives and doctor remain on the second. They work into the evening. Ray thinks of Soph, alone in the dome. He wonders again and again if he should drive and check on her, but there's nothing to do. You can't knock on an airlock door that is maybe a portal and ask to be let in.

It's a little after 8 p.m. and raining hard when the midwives descend. Ray rises from the couch.

"Help us pack our things, young man," says Bird.

"Is she okay?" he asks.

"For now," says Dr. Z. Gupta.

"Was it a miscarriage, or like *unnatural*..." He doesn't quite know how to ask if it's a parasitic alien baby grown from otherworldly seeds or dome effluence.

Rock steps forward. "A miscarriage is as natural as a birth," she says. "We celebrate one, fear the other, but both have their place, their reasons. Often the body makes decisions with its own good wisdom."

"Is…was…the baby… normal?" he asks.

"We don't judge," says Rock.

"No," says Toad. "We don't. But Iris will be okay. Dr. Z. Gupta will continue to run tests." She holds a small cooler in one hand, not unlike the cooler in which Ray totes his lunch to work. She lifts it to indicate that the things to be tested are inside. Something within, probably ice, shifts.

"Ray, the baby is still alive, it's still a viable pregnancy," says Dr. Z. Gupta.

"So not a miscarriage?" says Ray.

"There's nothing *mis* about it even if it was, young man," says Rock. "Iris's *carriage* is just fine either way."

Ray nods. "Okay," he says. He's always known these women to be a little cryptic, but he's also extremely tired and maybe not understanding.

The women look at him, brows furrowed. There's a faint sound from inside the cooler. A kind of scratching? It could be the ice melting and shifting.

"What's in there?" he says.

The cooler shifts and Toad loses her grip, grasps it with two hands to keep from dropping it. The lid pops off and a mess of ice and color-coded vials spill. They clank to the floor and roll every which way. The other midwives collect them.

Ray lets out a deep breath. He blurts it out: "I thought maybe there was a monster baby in the cooler."

"You're upset," says Toad. "And that's understandable."

Ray nods.

"Now go get our things," says Rock. "And carry them down. Quietly. Iris is sleeping."

•

When the equipment has been packed, when the midwives have left, Ray has a beer with Dr. Z. Gupta at the kitchen table. Ray tells him about Soph.

The doctor takes out his phone and sends a message. "Visitor will have a way. Another key. A plan. Something. Leave it until the morning. Soph has the RV. She's been there before. One night won't hurt her."

The doctor asks a lot more questions about what they saw and experienced in the domes. Ray tries to describe.

Whump.

Ray runs to the window. With the weather, he can't see much of anything on horizon. The wind is already blowing so hard he can't see or hear the ripple from the flattening. The doctor's phone makes a *ping-ping.*

"Wasn't Soph's dome," he says.

"Could be next time," says Ray. "We don't know if the flattening just cuts off access or…"

"Visitor has resources. Visitor is on it. There will be a plan in the morning."

"I should go to bed," says Ray.

"I hesitate to tell you, but there's a study," says Dr. Z. Gupta.

Ray doesn't have anything left in him but to stare blank-faced.

"Not conducted on humans. Not on this set of domes. So… more suggestive than anything. But." The doctor pauses. "When smaller mammals have had similar conceptions, the offspring fared better *within* the domes than without. Maybe because of stress. Maybe because of the epigenetic or genetic alterations that occur. In any case…"

"You want Iris to give birth inside the dome?"

"I wanted to give you the idea as an option."

"You did, or she did?"

"We did."

Ray can't make his brain work, can't figure out if this is good news—a plan—or just another Corpo-Agzone manipulation.

"We all want the same thing."

"To a point," says Ray.

"If I admit her to the medical facility. If she gives birth there.
I can't promise you they'll let you keep it. If they get the upper
hand—and I'd say it's neck and neck right now—I honestly don't
know what they'll do with you, with Iris, the baby, Soph."

"The counterparts? Visitor's enemies? Scrubland exile?"

The doctor nods. Stands up. "Time for us both to sleep, Ray.
My guess is I'll be seeing you all again tomorrow. It'll all be worked
out by then."

Ray lets the doctor see himself out. He turns off the kitchen
light and sits at the table in the dark, listening to the storm, watching how when the lightning flashes it casts giant shadows of win-
dow-raindrops on the wall. He's waiting for a *whump*. It doesn't
come. But he knows it will.

•

When Iris wakes around 10 p.m., Ray brings up a cup of herbal
tea for each of them and sits next to her on the edge of the bed.
His attention is divided. He wants to be here for Iris, but he's also
worried about Soph in the dome, alone. He's here, though, and
can't be there, and Iris needs him now. He tries to focus. "How do
you feel?"

"Scared," she says. "But a little relieved. The midwives have
their theory about miscarriage."

"As natural as birth, they told me."

"But I don't feel it in my soul. Miscarriage scares me. I want
to keep it."

"I know. And I want you to," he says, not knowing if it's entirely true. He wants it to be true. If it's human, or at least within
the ballpark of human, he thinks it's true.

She puts the cup of tea to her lips then moves it away. It's still
too hot to drink.

"But what if my body wanted to shed it for a good reason?

Maybe it's not natural at all to have this baby? That scares me."

He sips his own tea, not caring that it's too hot. He just doesn't want his own fear to show.

"Dr. Z. Gupta has a theory too," she says.

"Dome birth."

She nods, blows on her tea. "Dome birth.

"You're thinking, *yes*?"

"Soph will be happy about it. How is she?"

He takes another too-hot sip of tea.

"What's wrong?" Iris looks ready to jump out of bed and sprint somewhere, anywhere, to help her daughter.

Ray tells her what he knows. The note. The missing RV.

"I wonder what she's doing right now," he says. "Maybe sitting alone by a fire in the dark."

"We can't do anything until we get a new key. So, we have to trust Soph," says Iris. "She's probably a little scared, but this is something she wants. It's good for her to experiment with some independence."

"The domes are flattening. Visitor's enemies are doing it. One by one."

"We're not going to think of that until morning," she says. Her cup is trembling in her hand.

Ray takes the tea from her and sets it on the nightstand. He climbs into bed and holds her, the big spoon. It's been a long time since they've lain like this together. After a while she asks him to read to her.

It's a surprising request, and the book is even more surprising. It's a bodice ripper, the kind with a shirtless, muscular man on the cover. It's yellowed and dog-eared and most of the sex scenes are underlined. It was written long, long ago. He shouldn't be surprised. He's seen other books in the series and its infinite spinoffs lying around. The nurse-midwives and doulas of the practice circulate them and talk about them nonstop. Escape from the job, Ray imagines. A kind of antidote.

Ray reads. Raindrops tap the dark windows.

"Oh, Lorenzo," Iris says often enough that Ray learns to barely pause when she says it. She has many different kinds of *Oh, Lorenzo*. Sometimes it's a commentary on his foolish mistakes or on the fragility of his heart. Sometimes it's disappointment in his temper or naïveté. Other times it's wistful, with a little too much longing for Ray's liking.

The story rotates between Lorenzo's lovers' points of view, and Ray and Iris take it all straight-faced, in stride, with no laughter when narrators have orgasms that are described as avalanches, hurricane winds, ocean swells, and rays of light piercing dark clouds. It's a shock to Ray that, after what has happened, this is what Iris would want, but the more he reads the more this salve of escape makes sense to him. He feels it too. He never paid the books any mind, but for some time now this whole other world has been happening all around him.

"Oh, Lorenzo," says Iris.

Oh, Lorenzo, he finds himself thinking.

They take a break to pee, and Ray tries to call Soph for the third time, just to see if he can get through. He can't.

They spend the last few hours of the night reading about Lorenzo's muscles and the way he satisfies the narrators with his poetic words and acrobatic sex moves. It's late when Ray realizes Iris has been asleep for some time and he's been reading to himself. He tries to ignore a wispy seed puff clinging to the ceiling fan. He finishes the book and starts the next one. Finally, the first glow of Monday morning sunlight peeks over the distant sod fields. Time to find Visitor; time to get Soph.

•

Ray gets to work hours early, just before 7 a.m., but Golden Yolk is locked up. A weathered, creaky picnic table sits just beyond the parking lot, at the edge of the infinite fields of sod. Ray sits atop the table and drinks his coffee, eats a banana. He texts Gupta with no response. He texts Bob to come early, for an emergency. The late March air is a little chilly today, and the gusts blow right through Ray's jacket, but he doesn't mind. The cold arrests his endless thought loops, keeps him huddled, shivering, and out of the darker parts of his own mind.

Bob pulls up in his truck a little after 9 a.m., characteristically late, and waddles across the parking lot in a parka that hangs over his knees. A knitted stocking hat is pulled right down to his eyes. He waves a thickly mittened hand. "I heard. I heard all about it," he says. "Visitor is on it. We await her plan."

The tabletop creaks and wobbles under Bob's weight. His coffee smells of bourbon. Ray takes a sip when Bob offers. Bob lights up a cheap cigar and—in an obvious effort to distract Ray while they await the plan—chirps on about the latest antics of his wife, how she has him spring cleaning. "Not only did I mop the wood floors," says Bob, "but then I dried them with towels on my hands and knees. In my underwear! So that I wouldn't get my clothes dirty. That's how she wants it done. And before all that I sanitized the ceiling fans. I don't mean just dusted them off, but sprayed them down with a vinegar solution. *Sanitized* the fans!" They laugh about this. Ray can see that Bob enjoys it, enjoys doing these things, likes to show his love by doing chores for his wife that he'd never do for himself. "And now she's spring cleaning *me*," says Bob. "Look at my eyebrows! Look how trim they are. There's barely anything left. She took the clippers to them."

They laugh about Bob's eyebrows, which are indeed stubbly and severely over-pruned, and then they sit in silence, huddling against the gusts. Bob's cigar smoke wisps away as soon as it appears. Bob gets a text, reads it. Something shifts in Bob, Ray can feel it.

"Upstairs is doing something," says Bob. "They're all in a big meeting today. Things are off kilter." He takes the mug back and gulps a swig. He looks Ray in the eyes. "What I don't want you to do is to tell me if you've been letting eggs through. If that's the case, then I need to lie through my teeth to help you. But, Ray," he says. "I don't know if I can help you. Everyone eventually flinches. No one Egg-o-Scopes forever. I thought they'd move me out, move you up. But I don't even think they'll keep my position. I'm a leftover. I don't think the job will stay. I just wish I had a vision for you. It breaks my heart."

Bob places his hand on Ray's shoulder. Ray feels that Bob means it, feels genuinely bad. At the same time, Ray can't help laughing. Bob looks surprised. Ray hates to break it to him, but he does.

"No eggs?" says Bob. "No eggs? *No*. Really?"

"Not for the longest time."

"Then *what for*...?" He shrugs. "I suppose you don't know." Ray fills Bob in on the pregnancies. On the effluence. On Soph in the dome.

"The dome part I heard," he says. "Kid stuck in a dome. That's what I know. Asked me to help. *Of course*, I say. And...I'm a little scared, Ray. The lady made me an offer for my help today."

Ray raises his eyebrows.

"My wife is sick. Bad. We don't know exactly what. And, well, there are better facilities for diagnosing and caring in other places—not in other Corpo-Agzones, but in the actual cities. She said, well, you know."

"Help Visitor, get your wife in."

"But what are we getting into here?" Bob gets a text. Reads it.

"Some real deep shit, Bob," says Ray.

"Nope," says Bob. "Not shit. We used to think it was shit when we used to think the domes were for chickens. Now it's the effluence. Substation 9. That's where she wants to meet us."

"Shit Station? Where they sent Marc?"

"Effluence Station now, I guess. Doesn't have the same ring, does it? That's right. Flinchy old Marc is at 9. And I understand why she'd be out there. You should see how many assholes in suits went Upstairs to ransack her office."

•

Ray drives while Bob gives directions. The first direction is to steer the Toyota off the parking lot and right onto the expanse of grass. They drive alongside the row of old, defunct telephone poles that stretch as far as he can see. None of the poles have lines between them. Some of them are leaning or toppled. They drive for miles until Bob points out the glint of a beer can nailed to a pole. Here, they make a sharp right-angle turn and drive many miles more out into the wide-open ocean of grass until they see Processing Substation 9 in the distance, a terraced structure of cement. Viewed from the side, it looks like an enormous stoop the size of a building—like colossal concrete steps up to a giant's front porch, but without the house or porch. A big stairway to nowhere. Ray parks in the shadow of the bottom step.

Bob cups his hand to his mouth: "Marc!" He repeats it twice more.

"Up here," says a voice, not Marc's. Visitor's.

They take regular-sized cement stairs up to the first of the substation's terraces, which holds three rectangular lagoons. There are a lot of pipes and machinery between each body of water. They traverse a catwalk that passes closely over each of the three long pools. The first pool, which Ray assumes is the last stage of filtration, looks clean and clear—like you could take a dip and wouldn't mind if you accidentally swallowed a little. The middle pond, which disappears into a thick kind of dam before cascading into the final pool, is filled with so many floating plants and thatches of reeds that you can barely see the water. At the other end of the catwalk, right before the metal stairs to the next terrace, is a lagoon filled with pipes and pumps. It looks clear, but in places where the water swirls it looks thicker than plain water, maybe saline or chemically treated. Every few seconds the entire surface quivers.

Ray and Bob ascend the stairs. The substation's second tier looks exactly like a succession of shitty pools of water. They get progressively thicker and shittier. They wend their way up to the highest, final tier. Here, at the top, where the final terrace steps out into nothing, is a waist-high rail and a view across the endless organic lawn. It's sort of beautiful from this high up, the forever-sprawl of green to the horizon. An enormous pipe rises out of the field below, lifts above the substation, then curls down into the highest lagoon. A giant pipeline of chicken crap is what Ray once would've assumed, but it's whatever byproduct—whatever effluence—seeps into the ground from the domes.

Everything up on the top terrace smells like shit. There's a pumping noise that sounds like someone doing a bad Darth Vader impression. It's not the worst kind of shit smell, more barnyardy, earthy. But still shit. Between the two lagoons is what looks like Marc's living quarters, a little four-hundred-square-foot house plopped onto the cement. It looks out of place, with a pitched roof, shutters, and tiny front porch with a rocking chair and plastic flowers. Right outside the house, at a picnic table bolted into the concrete, sits Visitor in her characteristically fierce boots, long legs crossed.

Whump.

Ray and Bob dive to the cement and lay flat.

"Not there," says Visitor. She walks to the other side of the cesspool and crouches behind a metal box.

Ray only gets her meaning when the burst of air pressure shoots across the top of the substation, lifting muck off the pool and spattering it across Ray and Bob. As soon as it's over, Ray runs to the railing, looks out, and scans—as if he would even be able to tell if it was Soph's dome or not. Visitor smooths out her clothes and sits back on her bench.

"Your little girl's dome isn't scheduled until tonight," she says. "The little robots are setting it up while the big ones inside finish the harvest."

"Tonight?" says Ray. "Harvest?"

"How can I help you, Ray?" she says.

"She's still in there."

"The natural resources are worth a lot of money." She leans forward. "Do you see the shortsightedness of my counterparts? It's a world—a *world*, Ray. They want two-by-fours and minerals, but the scientific learnings, the medicines, the infinite possibility of infinite worlds." She shakes her head in disbelief.

"I need a key. Dr. Z. Gupta says—"

She holds up her hand. "I know. Give birth inside. Keep it. You're going to live in there."

"I don't know how long we'll stay. I guess it would depend on—"

She holds up her hand again. "Roy. Understand quickly. Not a question. I'm not asking but telling you: You're going to live there. You. Your family. I'll send the doctor. Bob. You'll survive better as a group, protect the baby. The baby is the mission. Dr. Gupta will collect the data. As able, I'll send for delivery."

Ray is trying to wrap his mind around it. It's kind of, sort of what he and Iris were entertaining, but it didn't seem fully real until now. "What happens when they flatten the dome? They're destroying them one by one. They've ransacked your office. You've lost."

Visitor is blank-faced, impossible to read. "How will you and Iris survive out in Scrubland amidst the sort that live there, Roy? With the girl in a flattened dome? The baby destroyed?" She smiles a half-pleased smile. "What's that feeling called? When your enemies feel like they're destroying you but are just helping cover your tracks?"

"I don't think *Ray* and I have had the pleasure of feeling that one," says Bob.

Thinking of destroyed people, Ray wonders where Marc is, and then he puts it together, understands about the pumping sound like a bad Darth Vader impression. A thick rubber hose passes between Ray's feet. One end is attached to the Darth Vader pump behind Ray. The other end of the tube disappears into the uppermost lagoon, atop which bubbles form slowly and break. It is attached to Marc, Ray realizes, who is breathing through it, deep down in the shit-smelling effluence, doing whatever his job is down there.

Visitor picks up a pouch from the bench, empties it on the table. A small pile of keys, maybe a dozen or so tadpole medallions. "We'll see if they're enough," she says. "My counterparts will be searching for them." She hands Ray two. "Take these, just in case. Bob, you and Gupta will have the rest. You'll need them inside. Ray, go home. Get Iris. Meet us directly at the dome door. A few of my guys will see that you get in, do what they can do."

"Lab guys?"

She scowls with something like disgust. "*My* guys."

"What time do we meet you?" says Bob.

She smiles: "You and Gupta are going in directly."

Bob frowns: "My wife…"

Ray sets a hand on Bob's shoulder. He feels bad, but he can't wait for the next *whump* that could be Soph's dome. He takes off at a jog.

"I've kept my word," he hears Visitor say behind him. "Your wife is a thousand miles away by now."

•

It's early afternoon when Ray delivers the news to Iris. She searches his eyes for what feels like a full minute, looking back and forth from one to the other, as if hoping to find some sign that he's not telling the truth.

"Then there's no time to pack anything," she says. "We go

now." She picks up Ray's hand, pushes the Toyota keys into his palm, and heads to the car. Both car doors are open and they're getting in when Iris freezes.

"What?" says Ray.

"Quiet," says Iris.

Then he hears it, the sound of tires speeding down the country road. They don't have their flashers on, but he can see them in the distance—the patrol cars of the Golden Yolktown security forces.

"Hurry—" Ray begins. He's imagining a car chase across the sod that will surely end with the patrol cars nudging their bumper, spinning them around, maybe flipping them, and…nothing good after that.

But Iris has already slammed her door shut, is already heading to the barn. Ray slams his door and follows her. She was a girl here. Played hundreds of games of hide-and-go-seek. She knows all the hiding places.

From their spot up in the hayless old hayloft, under a tarp, behind a pile of her dad's old restored junk, they can only listen to what's happening, not see. It's a lot of muffled shouting and stomping about in heavy boots and slamming of doors. After about forty-five minutes Ray's knees and back ache, but he doesn't dare shift position. Someone slides the barn door open. A flashlight beam sweeps and pokes the shadows. The someone shouts: "No RV."

They hear the sound of patrol cars leaving. They let a good twenty minutes of silence go by before they climb down from the loft, and every second of it Ray anticipates the *whump* that is Soph's dome. The gravel driveway is empty. No Toyota. Towed away.

"Dad's old Ferguson," Iris says.

"Ferguson," Ray agrees.

They run together to the barn again and pull the tarp off the old tractor. It's an antique, old-fashioned contraption with an autonomous driving system that, Ray remembers from his last spin, needs your hands on the wheel most of the time to actually keep it straight. Why you'd have a "self-driving" work machine you have to sit on and monitor, he's never figured out. It's barely different than doing the work yourself. When you let go of the wheel, he recalls, it spins back and forth, as if operated by a ghost. They hook up the battery. It blinks to life. It's made to look like a much older tractor, from way back in the two-stroke combustion engine days, but whether it actually resembles one or not Ray couldn't say because he's never seen one. They steer it out onto the sod with Iris basically riding on Ray's lap and point it toward the dome as the sun lowers in the sky. The old machine is faster than you'd think, clocking a steady twenty miles per hour on the grass.

•

Visitor waits for them at the dome airlock. "Her guys" are some kind of paramilitary outfit in tactical gear, helmeted, face shields down. They stand in a row, nine of them, and don't move. Ray assumes they're human, but…could just as easily be some kind of corporate tech he's never seen before.

"Cavalry," she says, nodding with her chin toward the sod fields behind them. In the distance, security force patrol cars race across the grass, lights flashing. "But not our cavalry."

She opens the airlock with a medallion, which she hands to Iris. "I'll disable the door when you're in so they can't follow, and then my guys and I will leave. No need to slaughter a bunch of barely trained locals with toy guns. Once inside, head over the ridge. Gupta and Bob have a head start. You have…" She grabs one of the soldier's arms and looks at his wrist tech. "Let's guess about two hours and forty minutes before *whump* time. You'll need to find her before then."

"And…what will happen inside, when the outside flattens?"

"You'll know before I do," she says. "I have an educated guess, but I'm curious to find out. Does it destroy a world or just disconnect the link?" She shrugs. "Don't know. But I would find her first."

Ray steps into the airlock. Visitor grabs his shoulder. "Not on foot. You'll want to take," she nods her chin at the Ferguson tractor, "whatever that piece of shit old lawnmower is."

•

The lights in the airlock flash on and off. The metal plates of the elliptical door spin open, and Ray and Iris drive the tractor into the world of the lake-in-the-dome. But it's not as they last saw it. There's not a single tree left, just a landscape of stumps. All the trees have been sawn off with extreme precision—not just flush with the ground but about an inch below it. The deep ruts and scrapes in the muddy earth look fresh. There's no sign of the night geese. The sawdust afloat on the lake is so thick that you can't see any water; it looks like an unusually flat stretch of land that someone might try to walk or drive across if they didn't know better.

Off to the side of the door, snug to the dome wall, is a stack of rocks with a fluttering note stuck between stones. *Robot machines sawing trees. Going deeper in. Past the lake. Over the ridge. To the other domes inside this dome.* The note is decorated with a little cartoon owl that has long been one of Soph's favorite doodles.

"She knew we'd come for her," says Iris.

They drive the Ferguson over the stump-pocked, muddy ground. At the top of the ridge, they look out over what may have once been a vast plain. It's unclear what might've grown here because it's now just a scraped-clean landscape of dirt and stone.

"Why would they tear up the land like that?" says Iris.

"Maybe strip-mined it for the topsoil?" says Ray. "So they can reclaim a little Scrubland? Or maybe they wanted a mineral near the surface? I don't know."

Scattered across this plain in nearly a semicircle are—Ray

counts them—eight domes.

"Why domes inside of domes?" says Ray. "Visitor's trick? Or… backup for the flattened domes? I can't figure it out."

"I don't have time to care," says Iris. "One Soph. Eight domes. Would she have left a sign somewhere?"

"Would a sign have survived all the digging and stripping and scraping that went on?"

"Look," says Iris, pointing. Way out on the wasteland is an enormous tank-like vehicle pulling an equally big trailer behind it. Both tank and trailer have treads instead of wheels. "The doctor and Bob."

They point the old Ferguson toward it.

•

When they are a mile or so from the vehicle it stops, slowly turns around, and drives toward them. A half mile from it, Bob pokes his head up from a top hatch and waves his arms.

"What in the world kind of setup did she send you in here with?" says Bob when they arrive, referring to the old tractor. They're all standing outside the tank, which is about the size of a small home, with the trailer about the same size. It looks like it would pass through the dome airlock with just inches to spare.

"Iris's dad's old tractor," explains Ray. "Long story for later. So, where is she?"

"The RV likely left clear, obvious tracks through grass or whatever was here before they strip-mined it," says Dr. Gupta. "She must've assumed we'd follow her path."

"That's a lot of confidence in the teenage brain," says Iris. "But maybe."

"She's a good egg," says Dr. Z. Gupta.

"No one ever talk to me about eggs ever again," says Bob.

"It's not exact," says the doctor, "but the dome that's the closest to straight ahead in the semicircle, we could call that one

Twelve O'Clock. We tried it, but it was basically a swamp inside.
RV would've been stuck within a few feet. But we saw shoe prints,
so we think she walked in, assessed, and walked out."

"Hard pass on Dagobah," says Bob.

Iris shoots him a *stop fucking around with nonsense* scowl, and
Bob flinches.

"How much time?" says Dr. Z.

"About two hours now," says Iris. "Tad more maybe. And yes,
I'm doing the math along with you. There's no time to search them
all unless we split up. Two vehicles, two groups. At least one group
has to reach Soph. We don't know what happens to this dome
when it flattens."

"Even if we go in, we still don't know what happens to internal
domes when their external dome flattens," says Bob.

"But are we in or out?" asks Ray. "When I looked back from
the ridge," says Ray, "the dome we came out of is a complete dome,
just like these internal domes. So, there's not a clear inside and
outside. We could just as easily be inside those domes as outside
of them—and our world could be inside or outside any of these
domes. It's unclear."

"No time," says Iris. "OK, Twelve O'Clock dome is done. The
four domes to our right we'll just call One O'Clock—Two, Three,
Four. Ray and I have them."

"Just a sec," says Bob, and he heaves himself into the open
door of the tank.

"Leaving Team B with Nine, Ten, Eleven," says Dr. Z. Gupta.
"We should do the closest—Eleven O'Clock and One O'Clock—
first. They'd be the easiest for Soph to get to from Twelve, and the
fastest for us to get to. Better odds."

Iris and the doctor nod in agreement. Ray nods too, but he's
already getting lost.

"Okay," says Bob, reemerging. "We are well provisioned.
Visitor got that right. Flare gun. Binoculars." He hands them to

Iris with a sheepish, nervous smile, maybe trying to get back on her good side by showing he's of use. They divvy up medallions. "Whatever team finds her, get eyeballs on the other team—so as not to miss us if we're in a dome—and shoot it high. Then, the non-flare team will haul ass."

Iris looks through the binoculars, using the laser sight to estimate distance. She puts the binocs down. Closes her eyes to think. "Not enough time."

"Are you sure?" says Gupta.

"I don't know," she says. "Wait." She closes her eyes again.

The doctor opens a notebook, starts to scribble. He sets it on the ground, and Iris squats beside him. When the doctor gets up to check distance with the binoculars, Iris takes over the pencil and paper. Ray hardly follows a single element of what Gupta and Iris do next.

"Eight miles per leg, rounding."

"Let's estimate twenty miles an hour, so twenty-four minutes."

"Yes, per leg. Four legs for Team A to search domes One through Four, then a fifth leg if they're the non-flare team and need to cross to the other side."

"That's ninety-six minutes for the legs. Cross adds thirty-five. Dome time is four domes—let's say twelve minutes, three inside each."

"Not enough."

"That's what I've given it. Keep going."

Ray steals a peek at the paper. Iris has laid out the semicircle of domes like a clock and is calculating the time and distance between them—as well as the time for one team to cross the entire landscape, the diameter of the clock, to the other side of the semicircle. Iris draws a long line from Four to Nine. Labels it *HAUL ASS.*

He hears Iris say it quietly: "Team A is at 143."

"Is Team A us?" Ray asks. "143 is over the two-hour limit, by a good bit."

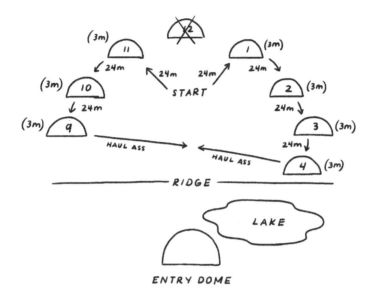

Gupta nods. "Unless you skip searching a dome. Or, ideally, if we find her before and Team A doesn't need to cross the diameter. But…there are multiple worst-case scenarios here in which you'd have to skip dome Four."

"What?" says Ray.

At high speed, Iris summarizes: "You and I have four domes to reach. But, assuming two hours, there's only enough time to search three in the event Team B fires the flare and we need to cross the plain to Nine."

"If we light the sky at Nine," says Bob, "you'd better already be moving."

"We already need to be moving minutes ago," says Iris. She runs for the tractor.

Ray glances at the map, sort of gets it. He follows.

•

They drive. Ray tries to ease the old beast over twenty miles per hour, but the tractor hates it, and he's afraid they'll break down or lose a wheel. When they hit One O'Clock, he assumes they've made it in twenty-four minutes, but he's not sure, and it doesn't really matter. *Fast* is what matters. But not so fast they wreck the tractor or twist an ankle. There's an old saying about slow and smooth being fast, but he's too panicked to remember it.

•

They place the medallion. The ramp and flashing lights and elliptical portal are all the same as their original dome, but when this dome opens up they walk into a kind of wild, haphazard apple orchard, overrun with dense, thorny vines. They call for Soph with no answer. The thicket looks impenetrable, and there's no sign of an RV passing through the bramble, which it would have to. They call it done. Searched. Was it under three minutes? Ray doesn't know.

The second dome is a frozen wasteland, so cold that no one would survive a half hour there. No wheels have driven through the snow and ice. Easy call.

At the third dome—*a charm* they call it optimistically, as they rush to the door—they place the medallion. Nothing happens. They switch medallions. Same. Only on the third try with a third key does the airlock rotate open. They don't talk about it, but it's clear what it means: Visitor's enemies are searching "the system" and turning off keys.

Inside is a pleasant coniferous forest carpeted in soft, fallen needles. Birds chirp. They call her name, but it becomes clear that their own feet are making obvious tracks and disturbances in the needles, and so would Soph's feet, and certainly the RV tires. They call it. Ray guesses it was more like five minutes, but they shaved off some time in the ice dome.

They exit dome Three O'Clock, and Iris looks across the wasteland to Nine. Ray hopes for a flare, meaning Soph has been found. But nothing. "Vehicle spotted, parked," says Iris. "But no Gupta, no Bob."

"So, they're inside the dome?"

"Should be out by now, or any second—they've had a little more time than us—but if we're going to cross, we need to go now. We have to choose: Four O'Clock or Nine O'Clock?"

"What does it mean that they're not there? Maybe Soph is hurt inside."

"Maybe Bob and Gupta got attacked by a pack of wild whatevers and are dead."

They both look across the waste at Nine. "You have to decide," she says. "I can't live with a wrong choice here."

"On the tractor," he says. "Go."

Ray presses the button. He drives hard toward Nine, pushing the speed. The tractor is wobbling and shuddering at about twenty-six miles per hour, shaving off seconds. He prays the tires stay on. Iris is trying to look through the binoculars, but Ray doubts she sees anything with all the bumps.

"Why Nine?" she shouts right in his ear, too loud.

"I don't know," he says.

Does he know? It'll be on him forever if he's wrong. Why did he make a decision at all? It's a feeling. He still feels it. What was it Visitor told him about his special accumbens and amygdala? His brain can see what the eye can't? It is maybe that kind of feeling. Should he trust it? If no, then there is still time for dome Four. His brain goes into berserker mode, and he imagines it shooting sparks and smoke inside. Maybe it is just that dome Four feels too easy—the hard drive for Nine against the clock feels more effortful, and in his mind a great effort feels likelier to be a success. He hopes not. It sounds like him, but: bad decision. Sometimes less effort is smarter. Was it that none of their domes seemed like a place Soph would want to live, so...maybe their side had the worse, less hospitable domes? But that wasn't true of the coniferous forest—dome Three was *exactly* the kind of place Soph would want to live. There it is. That's it: she never would've continued to Four. He knows his daughter. Dome Three would be her dome had she been there. Plus, *plus*: The other day, the day of the yellow eye, Soph had said something about being left-handed and making counterclockwise choices. Would she even remember saying that? If she exited Twelve O'Clock, looking back at the ridge, well…what would the right-hand or left-hand choice be? Hard to say. But counterclockwise still held true. That would mean dome Eleven would be her direction. Maybe it wasn't a great data point, maybe even a little stupid—but the beautiful pine forest was sound thinking. It was at least something to go on. And at least he had a way to explain his choice to himself if he turned out to be wrong, if he had incorrectly trusted his gut and lost his daughter forever.

·

When they get closer to the tank, Bob opens the sliding door and waves to them. The vehicle lurches into motion, toward the dome, with Gupta at the wheel. What have they been doing?

"What the hell?" Iris yells alongside them.

"No keys!" yells Bob. "Stopped working! We didn't want to make a decision, so we hid from you."

Ray guesses that Iris has a few more untried keys in her pocket. It's possible that they've all been found in the code and turned off. In which case…maybe they'd have made Four in time. Maybe all along this has been less a race against time and space and more against key discovery, which they hadn't counted on.

Iris runs from the tractor. Places a medallion on the reader.

The elliptical doors rotate open.

Iris runs in on foot. Ray speeds the tractor through after her, scraping the wall a little. At the last moment, he realizes Bob and Gupta don't have a working key and the tank and tractor can't fit in at the same time, since the tank and trailer are the size of a small house. He grabs keys from Iris and, as the doors close, he launches them. Before the teeth interlock, he sees Bob and Gupta, looking stressed, stooping to grab medallions. Then Ray realizes he's an idiot: they could've abandoned the tank and supplies, let the guys in the airlock. Everything is happening too fast. He may have just killed them.

•

Inside the Nine O'Clock dome, they see the RV tracks on the sand dunes immediately. They abandon the tractor—the sandy hill is too steep, they might tip over, and it feels right to run. They clamber over the dune as fast as they can, which is slowly. At the top, the salty wind strikes them. The waves of an iron-gray ocean crash hard on a beach strewn with shells. A voice calls back, and there she is, atop the RV, maybe a quarter mile down the beach. The cold salt wind whips their hair. The landscape instantly transforms from dreary to the most beautiful of all the dome worlds, for having Soph in it. They run to her. Millions of tiny seashells crunch underfoot. Soph climbs down the RV ladder. They embrace and all talk at once, unable to hear each other over the surf.

"You said you were with Dr. Z Gupta and Bob?" Soph yells over the wind.

The family hikes back to the dome. They place the medallion. The airlock opens, and wedged inside is the tank and trailer. Gupta drives it out.

"Holy shit," says Bob. "It went dark in there. I thought that was it for us, stuck between domes forever."

With the tank and trailer safely out, the door once again closed, they try the medallion again, just to experiment, to see if they can access the wasteland outside. The airlock opens. But instead of slow-blinking blue, the room blinks a rapid red that obviously screams "*danger.*" No one wants to venture into the airlock with both doors shut, stuck between domes, so they abandon the experiment.

"Maybe it's all flattened," says Soph. "Maybe there's no longer anything on the other side."

•

For a little while, maybe an hour, they are all elated: they are alive! Soph has been found! But then there's a sharp dip in energy. Now they're *here*. Bob without his wife. Gupta without his family. With nowhere else to go. Stuck. And they'll have to survive. No one is saying any of this out loud, but it's visible in the methodical but slightly irritated way they start to set things up and take stock of their supplies. Bob grumbles about the lack of cigars.

But also, they're hangry—and maybe sleep deprived, or dome-lagged. By the sun in the sky, it looks like it's before noon here, but—they all have different guesses—maybe after 8 p.m. back home. Not late, but…after a day like this, after experiencing multiple dome-days in multiple dome-times, they're wiped out. They make a driftwood fire to save on fuel canisters and heat up some of the food supply. They'll have to start scavenging the area first thing tomorrow.

As they eat, they all perk up. They're able to laugh a little, even if it's tinged with sadness. Soph excuses herself to run down to the beach. She's crouched down on the sand looking for something. Ray gets up to join her, and Iris takes the hint. The family needs a little alone time; it's uncertain how they're going to work that out in here long term. But Gupta and Bob seem to pick up on it and stay put.

"What do you see?" says Iris.

"I don't know," says Soph. But it's obvious what it is. A footprint. Bare. Five human-looking toes. "Maybe it's mine from earlier?" says Soph.

Ray hovers his foot over it. Smaller than his but not by much. "Not yours," he says.

"Is this a good thing or a bad thing?" says Soph.

All three look around, to see if there's a barefoot someone else
in the area. Just Gupta and Bob, struggling to pretend like they're
not noticing something going on. Sea foam spreads itself over the
shell-strewn sand, erasing the footprint a little more.

The family retreats to the sanctuary of the RV, which feels
more like home. They sit at the tiny foldout table in the kitchen-
ette. They open the RV's bigger side window and stare out at the
ocean.

"There's something big out in the water," says Soph. "Bigger
than a big whale. I saw it surface several times before you got here."

They all look out the window, but don't see anything now.
They tell Soph about Dr. Gupta's theory of dome birth, about the
deal with Visitor, about the security forces raiding their house. She
tells them about the distant sound of mech-tech that appeared
suddenly in their original dome, followed by the buzz of saws and
the crash of trees. She didn't stick around long after that, just left
the note in the rocks and fled over the ridge, where there had been
a plain of tall, golden grass.

"What's it like in there now?" she asks.

"Nothing left," says Iris.

"Big profit in that kind of lumber," says Ray. "I imagine. And
whatever they excavated."

"I thought you'd just follow the RV tracks in the tall grass," she
said. "Seemed foolproof at the time."

The RV rocks back and forth in the beach wind. Waves crash.
They all stare out the open window, all exhausted. A nimbus of
sunlight strains through the cloud cover. Ray tries to imagine the
days ahead, the hours ahead but, instead, his mind wants to picture all the other scenarios that might've been. He sees them in
their original dome, had it not been destroyed—the family gliding
in a canoe out to the misty island of the night geese. He sees them
escaped, with Visitor's help, to a different Corpo-Agzone, recreat-
ing a life close to what they had before. He sees them exiled out

to Scrubland, huddling in the cold, scared, afraid of who might find them. He sees himself in the bottom of a substation shit vat, like Marc, the reality of his shitty life sinking in as he breathes through a tube, looking out through a helmet window, darkness of effluence swirling around him. He sees himself if nothing had happened at all, back at his Egg-o-Scope, the same perfect egg before his eyes for a few decades more, until the end of his working days.

What he doesn't see, at first, is what Soph points to.

"There!" she says.

A sliver of sun emerges and transforms gray water into a vibrant blue green. Ray spots it, what Soph is showing him, way out there: a leviathan surfaces, spraying droplets of refracted color into the air. Its scaled back sparkles like gemstones. As it rolls, a flash of yellow, maybe its massive eye blinking open, or maybe just a flash of sunlight on scale. They pull each other close and look on in slack-jawed wonder at the shimmering beast, the rainbowed swirls of ocean mist. Soon enough, clouds will shift, gray seas and doubt and fear will resume. But right now they are together, a family that has traveled worlds to find each other, and they share a feeling that, like the undulating serpent, will still be there, swimming beneath the waves, always, even when they can't see it.

ACKNOWLEDGMENTS

DEEPEST THANKS TO EVERYONE at Dzanc Books, especially Chelsea Gibbons—for her generous questions, sharp insights, and incredible patience as I worked to apply them. And to Michelle Dotter, for her copyedits that helped refine the book from start to finish. I'm also grateful to the many behind-the-scenes folks at Dzanc. Thank you, all.

Thank you to my academic homes. Indiana University, where I fell in love with academe (cheers to you, Dr. Bilgarius). At Syracuse, early drafts took shape with the support of more teachers and peers than I can name. At the University of Cincinnati, where I got brave enough to be myself as a writer, special thanks to Brock Clarke, Michael Griffith, Leah Stewart, Peter Grimes, Soren Palmer, and Tessa Mellas.

Thank you to the jobs that sustained me. Naropa offered a warm literary home when I really needed one. Centre College, CIA, and Franklin College each shaped me as a teacher in different ways. Naked & Thriving, where I made the big shift from Professor to Brand Director. Thank you for your trust, Greg.

Thank you to the arts organizations that gave time, space, and belief: Saltonstall, Yaddo, Sewanee, the Kentucky Arts Council, Sarabande/Bernheim, the Indianapolis Arts Council, and the Taft Center.

To my friend and neighbor Barney Haney—thank you for the

conversations, encouragement, and for inviting me to speak with your students.

And to Jamie Poissant—you are a true-hearted friend, more than an aloof weirdo like me deserves.

To my family, above all: thank you to my sister and brothers—Sam, Aaron, and Galan. Thank you for the invented games and all the strange, sprawling versions of hide-and-seek we never finished. You shaped me.

To the Indy Moodys—Aaron, Alissa, Parker, and Izzie—your closeness and love have meant everything.

To my parents—thank you for making books central in my life, and to Cindy Cobb for your enduring kindness. Michael Kimball, thank you for all your time and attention to the kids.

And the grand finale—the brightest fireworks of love—belong to my Songbirds. May we reign forever in the wondrously weird little world we've made together:

Stella and Forrest—you are my heart.

Margi—I love you more than coffee and quiet. You are my true glade of magical trees, where I belong.

ABOUT THE AUTHOR

CHRISTIAN MOODY HAS BEEN PUBLISHED in *Esquire, Alaska Quarterly Review, The Cincinnati Review,* the *Best New American Voices* anthology, the *Best American Fantasy* anthology, and more. He received his MFA in Creative Writing from Syracuse University and PhD in English from the University of Cincinnati. He was a creative writing professor for many years, and currently works as brand director for an e-commerce company. He lives in Indianapolis with his two kids and wife, memoirist and illustrator Margaret Kimball.